STRAW DAMSEL

When her stepmother arranged an unwelcome marriage, Louise felt she must do something about it . . . because George was the most unpleasant man she had ever met . . . until she met the dark stranger in York and was accused of being a straw damsel, an insult she found hard to forgive.

Books by Emily Wynn
in the Linford Romance Library:

APRIL SQUIRE
CARTE BLANCHE

EMILY WYNN

STRAW DAMSEL

Complete and Unabridged

LINFORD
Leicester

First published in Great Britain in 1980 by
Robert Hale Limited
London

First Linford Edition
published November 1990

British Library CIP Data

Wynn, Emily
  Straw damsel.—Large print ed.—
Linford romance library
I. Title
823'.914[F]

ISBN 0–7089–6925–9

Published by
F. A. Thorpe (Publishing) Ltd.
Anstey, Leicestershire

Set by Words & Graphics Ltd.
Anstey, Leicestershire
Printed and bound in Great Britain by
T. J. Press (Padstow) Ltd., Padstow, Cornwall

1

"DO not be absurd, dear child! Of course, you must marry George! It is most fitting and proper. Now that your dear Papa is dead and your cousin, Eustace, succeeding to the title, he will need this house and I will live in London. What would you do otherwise?"

Louise stared from her stepmother to George, fat and uncomfortable in the background. He looked uneasy as if he, too, was being coerced into this hasty marriage. Old Mr Jennings of the desiccated appearance, who looked like a thin crow, nodded his head.

"I was your father's solicitor for many years, and I know he would wish to see you comfortably settled." He coughed delicately. "Dying so suddenly, he did not make arrangements . . . As the circumstances of your birth are, let me

1

say . . . unusual, I think as a defenseless young lady, you would do better to marry and put your considerable inheritance into capable hands."

"And you think George's hands are capable?" Louise spoke with more passion than was usual in a well-bred young lady barely twenty. But then her doting father, knowing he had done her wrong by not marrying her mother, had given her her head to the everlasting disapproval of her stepmother.

"Of course, dear George is quite capable. You are unmaidenly Louise, and should cultivate a watchful tongue! George, dear boy, tell Louise of your fondness for her, and that you offer for her with all your heart."

"Yes Aunt, of course Aunt. Er-er Louise, that is er, my love, I am willing, nay honoured to make you my wife . . . I think, I am sure, that I-er, could look after your fortune, and er-er protect you from all harm and, and-er, embarrassment as to your station in life!" He sounded as if he had tried to memorise the little speech, but had little enthusiasm for it.

"You mean you are willing to condescend to marry me?" Louise's voice was uncommonly sharp.

"Dash it all, haven't I just made myself clear?" George was both petulant and uncomfortable. He had no mind to have a long-drawn out discussion of the affair. If his Aunt Agatha said marriage to Louise was on the cards, marriage it would be, but he wanted to get back to his cock-fighting, he knew a man who had two cock-birds for sale, prime birds and going cheap. Looking at the slip of a female in front of him, he saw not her but the sleek lines of two well-trained grey-plumed cocks, and his pulses raced. He must get them before that blackguard Saunders knobbled them! He turned to leave the room.

"George! Where are you going? We must get this business settled and the contract signed." His aunt's strident voice stopped him in his tracks.

"I thought it was settled. I'm willing

to marry her." He muttered. "What more can I do?"

"Could you not show a little more pleasure, George? After all, we want Louise to be happy. Do we not, George?" She cast Louise a brilliant smile. "I must see my stepdaughter is happy. It is my bounden duty. Your dear Papa would . . . "

"I'll not marry George! Do not tell me what my dear Papa would have done. Spare me that Madam," Louise faced Lady Belgower with angry eyes.

Lady Belgower drew a deep breath. It had been the same for all of the five years she had been married to Sir Timothy. This antagonism from her stepdaughter who had a lively will of her own and was hard to browbeat. This time there would be no Sir Timothy to shield this-this by-blow, by a daughter of a draper, of all people! The thought made Lady Belgower's long nose curl up. Why he had insisted on keeping the child after the mother's death was beyond her, for he had lived as a bachelor all his days. Until the fateful day when she had first met him at the Playhouse in the company of her dear friend, the Marquis of Densburgh.

It had taken precisely two minutes for her to make her mind up to become the Lady Belgower. Better to be the wife of a country squire than the mistress of a fast-dwindling bankrupt! A marquis was a feather in any woman's cap — while the money flowed, but when it was finished, he was just as pathetic as any other man!

But the kindly Sir Timothy had proved surprisingly stubborn after marriage. His settlement on her had been generous but not too lavish. As he was all of twenty-five years older than herself, he had made provision for her on his death, but the surprising thing of all was that all the unentailed property and a goodly sum of money went to the chit, as Lady Belgower privately called her. The rest of the property went to the heir, Sir Timothy's nephew, Eustace.

Eustace! Lady Belgower remembered

the frosty reception she received from Eustace Belgower and his upstart wife, Maud. There would be no living at Belgower Towers with that couple! Her only hope was her own nephew, George Holdsworth. A boy she could lead and dominate. Her lip curled as she looked at him. If he ever succeeded in marrying Louise, the little nip-shot would have to pay for the privilege!

She looked Louise up and down, and her coldly angry glance made Louise shiver inside. She could remember when her stepmother punished her for trivial offences when her father was from home. What could she do to her now?

"You will go to your room and meditate on your remarks. Of course, you will marry George! I think it is a little maidenly prudishness that ails you. Think about it, and you will, I am persuaded, be more inclined for the married state."

"Never! I shall marry for love or not at all. I shall gladly go to my room. My own company is better than any I find here."

She looked proudly from one to the other, and George flushed an unbecoming red.

"Stap me! But I really believe she means it! Do you not want to become respectable? A miss like you should think of these things."

"You mean because I'm a bastard? And would marrying you make me respectable? I doubt it. I'll not be bought and sold like a pedigree cow!"

"Enough! Go to your room girl! You will not insult my dear nephew." Louise laughed.

"I shall go, and be pleased to do so, but as for your dear nephew, he is only dear when he does as you bid. I have heard you revile him as a stupid boy. He means nothing to you . . . Good morning Mr Jennings, it was a sad day when my Papa died." She left the room and, rather pointedly, slammed the door.

Lady Belgower looked from George to Mr Jennings.

"The dear child is distraught, and does

7

not realize what she is saying. She will come about."

"Lady Belgower, if Miss Belgower objects to an early marriage, and would like further time to consider." He coughed delicately, "another alliance, matters could be arranged." Mr Jennings looked hopefully at the lady's angry face.

"Nonsense, Mr Jennings. The marriage is arranged. A few days, and the child's shy scruples will be overcome. Leave us now Mr Jennings if you please, I have a mind to speak to George."

"Mr Jennings gathered up his papers and bowed, left the room. Outside in the great hall he was in time to catch Louise just beginning to mount the stairs.

"Miss Belgower, Louise . . . May I speak with you for a moment? I have been a good friend of your father's for years. If I can help you in any way, I should be honoured to be of service." Louise drew nearer. Her eyes were suspiciously bright. Mr Jennings put out a hand and covered hers.

"Thank you, Mr Jennings. I am in

sorry straits, but what I can do, I know not. How long is it before I can control my own fortune?"

"I am sorry Miss Belgower, Sir Timothy was most explicit. You will have to be twenty-five years of age and a confirmed spinster before being considered mature enough to control your own fortune. And then only on advice from the banker your father put in trust of your affairs."

"Then I am undone. My stepmother is a forceful woman. She may break my resolution and force that detestable marriage upon me."

"Forgive me for mentioning your circumstances, but what of your mother's people? Might not a relative of hers help?"

Louise looked at him, with a sudden hope in her eyes.

"My poor Mama! I had indeed forgotten about her! Perhaps there is a place in the world for me yet!" She smiled and Mr Jennings suddenly wished that he had been thirty years younger and not a crabbed old bachelor.

"Goodbye, Mr Jennings. Thank you for your kind offer, and I think you may have helped me already!"

She danced away from him, skirt flying and whisked up the stairs two at a time. Mr Jennings watched her go in disapproval. Shaking his head, he wondered at the modern miss and her hoydenish ways. And yes, he was sure he had seen six inches of ankle and leg. Miss Belgower was in need of a husband, if only to subdue that wild spirit. He took his well-worn beaver from the hovering footman and allowed himself to be escorted to the door.

In her bedchamber, Louise looked around at the room she had known since early childhood. The large dark oak furniture and the four-poster bed with the scarlet and gold curtains and overspread were part of her world. It was now, as if she was memorising the whole, a foreboding of goodbye.

Molly, the teeny maid, was blowing the coal fire with the bellows causing the chimney to belch smoke. Coughing and spluttering the little mob-capped wench tried desperately to create a through draught.

"'Tis blocked I think. That dratted chimney-sweep 'asn't done it properly. I said when I saw 'im, that newest lad 'e 'as doesn't know 'is job. 'e only looked about six, a puny skinny kid wi' red-rimmed eyes. It's not my fault Miss. I'm doin' me best."

"Never mind, Molly. I have other things on my mind. If it's alight, you may leave it."

"But if me Lady finds out, I'll be sent 'ome! Ma needs the two shilluns every week to buy bread, now she's near 'er time. I dunno where'll we sleep another. Me sister Emmy will 'ave to go out to a place. She's eleven, and I daresay strong enough to carry coal-buckets." She looked scared.

"Oh very well, stay there quietly. I'll not get you into any trouble."

"Thank you, Miss. If I goes down-stairs, Cook will give me all the pans to wash and polish. I 'ates polishin'." She crouched by the blackened fire which gave off little puffs of smoke, and held out her hands to the meagre warmth.

Outside, it was a typical November day, with fog and a glisten of rime. Louise shivered and drew her shawl tighter around her. The round low neck of her gown was pretty, and her chestnut hair gleamed in ringlets drawn away from the sides, but the thin stuff of the gown was no match for the cold of North Yorkshire.

There was the noise of a horse walking over cobbles. She rubbed the window-pane to see and could just make out the form of George Holdsworth appearing fatter and bulkier in a coat of many capes. His horse, big and heavy to carry such a man, moved stiffly and slowly down the carriageway. Louise fervently hoped the horse would take fright and unseat his rider. She smiled mischievously at the thought.

Turning from the window, she pondered on Mr Jennings' suggestion. There was an old carpet-bag in the back of the cupboard that had belonged to her mother. Until now she had not been curious about its contents. Her place had been secure with Papa. There had been no reason, other than the presence of the hated stepmother to worry her. She determined to get out the old carpet-bag and see if there were any indications of her mother's family.

But she was interrupted. Her stepmother came into the room and at once ordered the quaking maid to leave.

"Lud, the room has as much smoke as a blacksmith's! If you cannot light fires young Molly, we must find someone who can!" Her gimlet eyes raked Molly up and down. "Tell Mrs Twye to find you employment in the kitchen." Molly did a quick bob, and with a choking sob, rushed out of the room.

"It is not Molly's fault. The sweep's new boy is without experience. The chimney is partly blocked."

"Probably displaced some bricks. But that is not why I am here. I have spoken to George and he is willing for a wedding in one month. In the meanwhile, you will stay close to your room. We do not want you to be exposed to any sickness before the event, do we?" She gave Louise a brilliant, false smile. "I shall write to my mercer in London and have them send patterns of cloth for your wedding garments. No one shall say I did not do you pretty."

"But Stepmother, I have told you — "

"Not another word. Do you want it known that you would jilt your future husband? I am sending an announcement to all the leading news-sheets of the forthcoming marriage. You are a very lucky girl — in your circumstances. A man of George's birth may have refused you, on birth alone, but George is kind and very taken with you."

"You mean he is willing to obey orders."

"If you like, but it makes no difference. Now, to keep you safe I intend to lock you in Miss. And you will stay so until you change your mind." The hard face showed determination and for a few wild moments they stared at one another eye to eye, and then Louise's eyes dropped.

"You would keep me prisoner?" Her voice was low and charged with emotion.

"If you would like to put it that way. But marriage to George can only do good. It will settle your status in society, and later, if you must, you can take a lover. Provide George with an heir and you can go your own way!"

"Never! I should rather die!"

Lady Belgower shrugged.

"Be as melodramatic as you like. You will change your mind before you leave this room."

No sooner than the words were spoken, than she whisked out of the door, and it was slammed and Louise heard the rasp of the key in the lock. At once, panic seized her and she beat on the stout, oak door until she fell back exhausted and sobbing. But there was silence without and Louise guessed that the maids would be under orders to keep away from her room.

Weeping over, she took stock of her

15

situation. Again, she remembered the old carpet-bag. She found it under a welter of discarded and outgrown dolls and other well-loved toys. All proof of her Papa's affection for her. She picked out from them a wax doll of French origin dressed in court clothes and a little wooden doll with highly painted cheeks in mob cap and gathered skirt and fishu. They were her favourites. If it was possible to get away, she would take them to remember Papa.

The carpet-bag at first proved empty. Then riffling in the bottom and half-concealed by the torn lining, she found a small bundle of papers tied with ribbon. Curious, and half-frightened of what she was about to learn, she opened them with some trepidation. At first, nothing made sense. One or two of the papers proved to be letters from a man called Tyndal, very austere and formal. They were full of reproach and recriminations, and with some astonishment Louise realized they were from her mother's father. Reading them through again, she now could understand the gist of the rather wordy epistles.

They were full of repressed anger and Louise imagined the distress they must have caused her mother.

'For me, the name of Almira Tyndal ceases to exist. I am without kith or kin, a lonely old man who thanks God, that my good wife does not live to see this day. But for the past fondness I did bear you, I send by carrier all your earthly belongings and five gold sovereigns, and God be with you when it is your time to deliver your child. Yours in sorrow, Josiah Tyndal.'

Louise' hand trembled as she opened the second and third letters. They too, showed there was no forgiveness to be had, and also perhaps the reason Sir Timothy did not marry her luckless mother. The last letter had been a reply to a plea from Almira to come home. Sir Timothy was away on the King's business and she had been turned away by Sir Timothy's housekeeper. He did not know of the coming child that was evident by Josiah Tyndal's reply.

'What mishap befalls you is no concern of mine. Where you stay is of no consequence to me. You have conducted your business badly, and you should have acquainted your lover with the true state of affairs at the outset. I am sending you two pounds for your lying-in. Be sure to engage a good midwife but do not trouble to give me notice of the child. I want naught of it. Yours in sorrow, Josiah Tyndal.'

Louise bit her lip. How could a father treat his daughter so badly?

She remembered her Papa's halting explanation, when she had been old enough to be curious about her mama and her birth. Her Papa had not wanted to talk of it, and forbade her to mention her mother's name again. He had come home from abroad, and as he stepped down from his coach, the young girl he had loved, staggered forward, unkempt and dirty. She had hung about outside for days, awaiting him. Shocked, he had taken her inside and cared for her. But a month afterwards, she herself had been born and her mother was dead of child-bed fever.

There was a birth certificate, signed by the Parish priest, to wit, a daughter born to one, Almira Tyndal, spinster, age nineteen years, father unknown. The hand of the old priest had been shaky, and the date, October 7th 1792, hardly decipherable.

With suddenly shaking hands, Louise smoothed out the yellowing papers. For the very first time she felt a wave of emotion for that unknown mother — a young girl, a year less than she was herself.

Until now, her life had been pampered by an adoring parent. True, life had been less secure since the advent of the new Lady Belgower, but her quiet life and the cosseting had lulled her into thinking she would always be a lady of consequence.

Now, it was brought home to her that it was only Sir Timothy's goodness of heart that had given her a place in the world.

She shivered. Her world was suddenly chill and unfriendly, but her mind was made up and her spirit rallied. She would never marry that fat nincompoop George!

She scanned the rest of the contents of the bag. There were pitifully few signs of her Mama. A journal started, however, at the time she had first met Sir Timothy, was the only indication of her real self. She spoke of love, of Sir Timothy's kindness and her parent's disapproval. How she lived from one meeting to the next. Of her fears that he would be called away by the King on royal business. There was reference to the shocking French Revolution and its consequences. Above all, was the overriding fear for Sir Timothy's safety. Then came the dawning realization that she was with child and the loneliness now that Sir Timothy had finally gone. Gone without previous warning. Just a message sent by manservant to their trysting place.

Tears blurred Louise's vision. It was

increasingly difficult to read the last agonizing entries. How at last old Josiah Tyndal had challenged her. The scene when she confessed and her father's fury. The unhappiness and fright when she was ordered to leave her home. There were few entries for the next few weeks, but what there was left Louise in no doubt of the degradation her Mama had suffered. Then the last entry, and the evident delight of meeting her lover again and her concern of his wound and haggard looks.

Louise riffled through the book, but there was nothing else. No mention of the baby. Nothing. She felt a little hurt that her Mama had not thought her important enough to write down her impressions of her child. Then considering, remembered with compassion that her mother had died within a month of her birth.

Bundling the papers and the dolls back into the carpetbag, she added a few essential items of her own. Her reticule when searched held three pounds and seventeen shillings and a few pennies.

She placed the bag back inside the cupboard. She was ready if a chance arose to escape.

The hours passed. Louise spent most of the time under the feather quilt on her bed. The fire had died down and the room was chill. Then there was the sound of a key in the lock and Lady Belgower entered with a scared Molly carrying a well-loaded tray. Her stepmother gave her a grim look.

"Well, my girl? Have you come to your senses yet? Must you play the heroine, like a veritable Mrs. Siddons?" She tapped an impatient foot. Louise glared at her from the depths of the four-poster, but did not reply. "Very well then, I take it you are still being unreasonable. Molly, let the tray down and retire."

Molly made slow work of it, narrowly missing over-setting the tall jug of fragrant chocolate.

"Clumsy wench! I have a mind to cast you off. Leave it. Miss Louise will not require your services further."

"But Ma'am!"

"I said retire!" Molly gave Louise a last despairing look and shuffled out of the room. "Now Louise, I want no more nonsense. I have here the contract. I want you to sign. it without more ado." She placed the large document before Louise. "Here is a quill and ink. Do it now."

Louise took the stiff document off the feather quilt and looked at it through misted eyes. Her heart thumped. Now there was going to be a battle of wills. She was afraid. Sir Timothy had always been a restraint to her stepmother. She had never before experienced her full disapproval. She raised her chin.

"I see that you are in control of my money after my marriage until I am twenty-five and after that it reverts to George. Is not that a little unusual?"

"George is unused to looking after a fortune. It will give him time to adjust."

"But you assured Mr Jennings that George was quite capable."

"And so he is — up to a point. I only do this in your best interests. After all, you want to remain in your present position do you not? A respected lady of gentle birth and consequence?"

"And if I do not?"

"Then you would be a fool! But I am persuaded you would never do anything to sully Sir Timothy's name!"

"I honour my father's name, Lady Belgower, and would never do anything to dishonour it," she said quietly.

"Good! But why the formality? I am your loving stepmother. You must treat me so. Our friends — "

"Stop! Let me finish. You are my stepmother. Not loving mark you, but in the eyes of the world my stepmother. Legally, I am no relation. Remember? For that fact I thank God! I have loathed you ever since I first saw the hurt in Sir Timothy's eyes. You were never a good spouse to him who deserved the best. I, for one was not deceived by your smiles and social graces! I beg leave to tell you now, once and for all. I shall never marry your nephew!" She drew a gasping breath, preparing herself for she knew not what kind of fury.

Surprisingly, none came. Lady Belgower drew herself up. Her demeanour was cold and she held back the tide of rising anger.

"Very well," she said with ominous calm. "We both know how we stand. I shall remember your words and your opinion of me, but nothing is changed. You will remain here until you change your mind. And that I promise you, you *will* do! With that, she left the room, slamming the heavy door behind her and the key rasped in the lock again.

With hands that trembled, Louise lifted the lids of the tureens. The smell of oxtail soup, even growing cold, reminded her of a healthy hunger. Cold beef and a thick slice of ham surrounded by buttered parsnips and pickles tickled her palate. There was a curd tart, spiced and succulent to follow, and the comforting hot chocolate. She ate well, excusing herself on the grounds of keeping up her strength. A thin, snivelling creature would be no match for Agatha Belgower!

Replete, and with the courage that comes with a full stomach, Louise reviewed the situation. She remembered Mr Jennings' advice. Would her Grandfather Tyndal be still alive? And how, if he *was* still alive, would he react to a granddaughter he had never recognized in the first place? Another thought struck her. Perhaps there were other relatives? She took heart.

One thing was certain that Mr Jennings could not give her any material help. He was most certainly under Lady Belgower's thumb! Her thoughts cast around to their immediate neighbours. There was literally no one she could approach. Always providing she could escape, that is. Sir Timothy had led a secluded life in North Yorkshire, perhaps because he had been very aware of the disapproval of keeping a bastard child in his establishment! Gentlemen usually paid for their offspring to be looked after elsewhere, and therefore were no embarrassment to them.

Louise bit her lip. She had never

stopped to consider Sir Timothy's actions before. Her stepmother's malicious remarks had, for a long time, been only half-understood and then later, were put down to pure dislike. Now, she understood as if a flimsy curtain had been torn down. Papa must have loved her Mama and then herself, very, very much.

She must have slept, because awakening before daylight, she lay listening to the chimes of the old clock. Six o'clock! She threw back the bedcovers and ran to the window. She rubbed the small diamond panes, leaded and slightly distorted, but no moon showed, so opened the window to see what kind of a morning it was. Doing so, she looked down. She remembered the espalier pear that grew on that wall, but the leafless branches with their pointing arms were too far away from her window. No escape that way! But the morning was clear and dry. No sign of fog.

She shut the window quietly and hastily. It was cold, and not withstanding her high-necked night-rail felt chilly. She jumped back into the huge feather bed and covered herself again. She would wait for Molly lighting her fire before rising, but would Molly be allowed to light it?

The next two hours passed quickly enough. She dozed, and started up several times, each time thinking Molly was coming. But the morning was far gone when she realized no one was coming. She dressed without help. It was a struggle and she was shivering with cold when she finished. There was not much water in the ewer, but she washed her face and hands, shrinking at its freezing chill. She huddled into her thickest shawl and waited. Now she was hungry.

But no one came. By straining her ears, she could hear muffled sounds down below. She kept watch by the window, determined to shout and scream if visitors came by. There were no visitors.

Desperate, she hammered on the door again, and listened. Again nothing. Panic rose again within her. She was friendless. Why must dear Papa die in his sleep?

Now she was suffering pains in her stomach. She could not remember being so hungry in her life. A slow burning anger helped her to endure it. The more she was made to suffer, the less chance of her doing what her stepmother wanted! Then she heard the rattle of the coach and the clip-clop of Sir Timothy's chestnuts. The coach was coming round to the front of the house!

Watching from the window she saw Lady Belgower come out and descend the steps and Goodge the coachman hand her into the coach. She was dressed for an evening out. Louise drew a deep breath. Tonight would be the right time to escape, if only there was the means!

Pacing up and down the room, Louise tried to plan. It was difficult with cold and hunger seeping away her courage. When darkness fell, she lit her one solitary candle. She reckoned on about two hours light and then she would have to settle down again for the night, if she could not devise any means of escape.

She lay on her bed for a while, and then was aware of a steady scratching. Rats? She started up in alarm, but then realized it came from the door. Swiftly, she ran with bare feet across to the door and knocked back.

"Who is it?"

"It's me, Molly, Miss. Are you all right?" The whisper was hardly discernible.

"Oh Molly! Bless you Molly. Can you get me out of here?"

"There's no key Miss. I've worrited about you all day. They wouldn't let me light your fire and Cook had orders not to send up any breakfast. Oh Miss, what shall we do?"

"Lady Belgower is away from home. I heard the coach leave. Can you find the key and let me out?"

"Oh Miss Louise, I'm frightened. Lady Belgower do say as 'ow I'll lose my place if I don't do as she says. If you escape, I'll be blamed."

"But you wouldn't want to stay here if I was lucky enough to get away?"

"Oh Miss, it's me Ma. She needs the money. Pa's only a farm labourer, and there'll soon be nine of us!"

"Molly, find the key and I'll give you a pound for your Ma. That is ten weeks' wages. And when I get to London, I shall see that you get some more money. Help me, and I'll help you."

"Could I come with you Miss?" she breathed. "You've always been kind to me. When you get situated I could look after you."

"But I do not know what kind of a situation I shall be in! I cannot foresee whether I shall be able to afford you! I will not be a lady of consequence any longer. You know what is being said?"

"Aye, but it makes no matter. A lady you always will be to me."

"Then hurry and find that key! Every minute counts."

"Very well. Cook and the maids and the footmen are at supper. The housekeeper and Miss Biddle are supping in the housekeeper's room. They are friendly and when Lady Belgower is out for the

31

evening, the gin-bottle comes out!"

"Oh, so that's why Lady Belgower's dresser is always missing on those occasions. I often wondered. Now hurry."

There was silence, and Louise knew that Molly had made her way along the back stairs and corridors to the kitchen regions. She was gone a long time, until Louise despaired of getting away. Then came the scratching again. Molly's voice was hoarse with excitement.

"I've got the key, Miss!"

"Then for Heaven's sake, open the door!" There was the scrabble of a large key in the lock. It turned with a jerk and Louise heard Molly gasp. Then the door opened and Louise saw Molly's scared face in the light of a candle set down on the floor beside the door. "Miss Biddle had the key! I heard her boasting to the housekeeper about being my lady's right-hand. And she told her where the key was, and how she had not to give Miss Louise any supper! Here, I've also brought you some bread and cheese and the remains of a pigeon-pie, and the decanter from the dining-room. A drop of Madeira will bring your colour back Miss. You look very pale."

"Oh Molly, I'll not forget this, ever. Bless you." She tore into the food like an animal. It seemed much longer than one day she had gone without food. She took a long pull at the decanter, and then burped. Molly watched her anxiously.

"You be careful Miss. You'll not want to be foxed when we get away. You've taken rather a lot, and on an empty stomach."

"Empty no longer, Molly. I feel fine now." She hiccuped and stretched. "I'll get my carpet-bag and put on my warmest clothes. Help, me Molly, and you shall choose something warm too." They moved swiftly and soon they had a stuffed carpet-bag and two tied up bundles.

"I went and found Ned in the stables. He's a good lad and easy to manage. He has a fondness for me." Molly giggled. "He thought I'd gone to play around in the hay. I've persuaded him to harness the governess-cart to old Nellie, and drive us over to my Ma's. We can stay the night there, and tomorrow being Wednesday there is a mail-coach due at the Royal George at nine o'clock sharp. It stops at York, being the first stop from Richmond."

"Molly! I did not know you had the gift of conspiracy! You are being a wonderful help to me. Let us away and find Ned."

They crept down the backstairs of the mansion. Louise felt her heart quicken as they neared the servants'quarters. Miss Biddle would certainly try to stop her, and perhaps some of the other servants. Many were Londoners imported by Lady Belgower. They grumbled at their exile from London, but would all be loyal to Lady Belgower in a crisis. The country wenches who did the actual hard rough work of the mansion were too simple and easily swayed by the least note of authority by the other, more sophisticated servants.

Outside at last, Louise breathed the crisp cold air with relish. It was like being brought back to life. She thanked God for the dry cold which would make the roads passable. They had locked the bedroom door again and Molly had replaced the key, so that if Lady Belgower's instructions were the same, it could be far into the new day before she was missed. The coach could be well on its way to York, where they could change for the south-bound Post-chaise to London.

Ned had the old horse harnessed and was waiting in the stable-yard, nervously listening for any intruder. He wanted to be away and back before Mr Goodge the coachman returned with Lady Belgower. He dreaded any of the other servants hearing anything untoward going on in the stable. There was always someone waiting to fill a vacancy if a servant was turned off.

With more haste than courtesy he handed Louise and then Molly and their bundles into the governess-cart, and then leading Nellie, took a roundabout tour of the stables, coming out on to the carriage-way nearer the winding road that led to the village of Moresby. Then judging he was far enough away from the house, and any spying eyes, he jumped up in front and exhorted old Nellie to a reluctant trot.

Soon they reached the tumbledown cottage that Molly considered home. Ned deposited their bundles and the carpet-bag and not staying to see if they would be welcome, drove off at a fast trot. So intent was he, that he did not stay for a last farewell with Molly. She watched him go with tears in her eyes.

"So that's what all his fondness was worth! Too frightened of his own skin to wish us well. Huh! I'm mortal pleased I was too stubborn for 'im. Many's the time he's begged me — , and I wouldn't! Ma's face always came between us, and all those babies!"

"He thought enough of you to risk being caught with the governess-cart. He's got to get safely back yet. I think he has done marvellously well."

"Aye, let's hope nothing goes amiss,

or else he'll tell all he knows. He's too addle-witted to think fast. And then we would be taken back before morning."

It was a while before the knocking brought any response, and then the barred door was opened and Molly's mother blinked at them with the light of a candle.

"Oh, it's you, our Molly. What brings you here? Eh, and Miss Louise too. Come in do, and I can shut this door. The wind's that cold." The door banged to and the wooden bar slotted to fasten it from the inside. "Now lass, let me look at you. You haven't done wrong up at the big house? Mind you'll get a thrashing from your Pa if out is wrong."

"Nay Ma, nout's wrong. I'm helping Miss Louise. Where's Pa? Is he in?"

"Down with early lambs. Two ewes looked promising this morning and he's gone down to look flock over. He'll not be back till dawn."

"Good. Me and Miss Louise want to stay all night."

"Are you mad? Miss Louise can't stay

in the likes of this place. It's not fitten."

"Mrs Pendleton, I assure you Molly and I are not mad. She's been a wonderful help to me and you should be proud of her. For reasons I cannot go into now, I must go down to London to find my Grandfather. Molly wants to accompany me. We are going to catch the coach at the Royal George tomorrow and would much like to stay here overnight. Please say yes, Mrs Pendleton."

The woman looked amazed, and then turned to Molly and then again to Louise.

"But what of her situation? She was a lucky girl to get a good place and to live in and eat regular, and the money — " Her voice tailed off. Suddenly she looked weary and tired. "I 'ad 'oped she would stay and mebbe get Emmy a like situation. 'Twould be a feather in my cap to 'ave two daughters in good service. There's them in the village who thinks the Pendletons aren't good enough. And now." She sighed.

"Mrs Pendleton, I want you to take

this sovereign. It is equivalant to ten weeks wages for Molly. When she and I get to London, I shall arrange for you to receive some more money. Meantime, could we rest? We have a long way to go tomorrow."

"But where to sleep? As you see, the children are bedded down here. Up in the loft is Pa's and my bed, and a truckle bed for little Tom and Bert. There's nowhere else."

"We'll lie by the hearth till morning. The hearthstone is still warm. If we wrap ourselves well up in our shawls and lie together, we shall do well enough."

"'Tis poor hospitality to offer you, but it is the best I can do."

"Say no more, rather this than to be imprisoned in my own home." Mrs Pendleton's mouth was an O of surprise. "Yes, this is so, Mrs Pendleton. Lady Belgower is no friend of mine."

"Aye, there's been talk in the village. It was a bad business when Sir Timothy died." She brought out a thin grey blanket, not over-clean. It smelt as if

39

a sick piglet had been wrapped in it, but Louise was past caring.

Molly curled up like a young kitten and promptly fell asleep, snoring gently, but Louise stayed awake, long after Mrs Pendleton climbed her ladder to her bed.

For a long while she lay listening for the sound of horses clip-clopping along the road. It would mean that Ned had not stabled Nellie without being detected, but as the hours passed and there was no outcry, she was nearly certain that she would not be missed. After an evening out, Lady Belgower slept until noon, and it would please her to think that Louise was suffering from hunger and neglect.

She relaxed, and as her eyes closed in sleep she smiled. She would so like to have been there in spirit when Lady Belgower found that her prisoner had gone!

Wednesday morning proved fine, and after a bowl of thin porridge each, and a lecture to Molly from her mother to be a good girl and resist the temptations of London and look after Miss Louise, she waved them a tearful goodbye and promised to say nothing to Pa as he was not to be trusted for talking in the alehouse. A good thing, she said that he was out all night with the flock.

The cottage, being on the outer edge of Moresby, was soon left behind and a short cut through the fields got them on the road to Richmond. They could see the castle on its hill, and the winding River Swale meandering through verdant pastures and wooded hills. The carpet-bag was heavy, but Molly, sturdier than Louise and used to carrying heavy burdens made light of the two bundles.

Where they could they walked through the fields. The narrow winding roads, with dry stone walls on each side were in some cases too rough for easy walking. Deep ruts caused by heavy clumsy carts were half-filled with water from recent rains. Besides, they were fearful of who might be pursuing them. It was better to hide when any traffic approached, but apart from a man with a load of turnips in a cart drawn by a tired-looking grey gelding and the Vicar of Moresby astride a cob, there was no other traffic. They made good time, and apart from Louise's legs aching at the unaccustomed exercise, they came to no harm.

In Richmond, they found they had more than thirty minutes to spare so Louise resolved to speak with Mr Jennings. His house was one that overlooked the square cobbled market-place. She had been several times before with her dear Papa. Now, she did not hesitate.

Her ring at the bell brought the pleasant-faced housekeeper. Yes, Mr Jennings was at breakfast. She would enquire if he would receive the two young ladies. It was only a minute or so before he himself, came to the door and ushered them in. He offered them coffee, which they gratefully accepted and some fresh bread and butter and several slices of cold beef.

And while she ate, she told Mr Jennings of what had occurred. Mr Jennings then wrote a letter for her to present to her grandfather if she should find him, explaining certain matters as to reasons why Sir Timothy had not married Almira Tyndal. And also how Louise was placed. Then he gave her a purse with ten gold sovereigns in it, and besought her to hide them away from pickpockets, slick-tongued Johnny-cum-nightlies, or any other rabshackles. Louise's eyes flew open. It sounded a dangerous place, this London that she had only heard about and never visited. Perhaps running away to London was not as easy as she had first thought!

Then Mr Jennings accompanied them back to the Royal George and now the cobbled yard was full of activity. The post-chaise was in, and two ostlers were changing the panting steaming horses for a fresh team. Two passengers were leaving the coach, to find refreshment inside. Another passenger with large band-box was swarming up to get an outside seat.

Mr Jennings paid their fares to York

and saw them settled comfortably beside a stout, grey-haired lady who had trouble with her breathing. She gurgled and rattled as if just getting over a bout of lung fever. Inside, the coach smelt of dirty upholstery, human sweat and stale spirits. Louise shuddered slightly. It was the first time she had travelled by public coach.

Molly was excited and all agog. She clutched her bundle as if it would be filched from under her nose. And still the activity was going on outside. Tap-men came running, foaming pewter tankards spilling over in their haste. The coachman and his mate drank deep. The outside passengers, unwilling to leave their seats for fear someone else took their place, leaned over and took the proffered ale. Piemen came around in white aprons shouting, "Hot mutton pasties, just out of the oven, gents and ladies," and the stable lads unharnessing the tired team, rubbing them down with swathes of hay and then leading them away to the comparative warmth of the stable to be fed and watered. There were yells and shouts and the screams of a serving-wench who was being chased by a young popinjay in blue velvet jacket, grey pantaloons and a tall hat. His tall hat falling in the mud and muck of the yard, and Louise laughed aloud. Serve him right for molesting the pretty girl in the rather dirty white apron, even though she did not appear to be as frightened as she should have been!

At last, all were aboard. The coachman drew the ribbons through his fingers, the guard gave a mighty blow on his long thin horn, the outside passengers gripped their safety handles hastily, and after giving a display of cracking the long leather whip, the coachman gave a great bellowing "Gee-hup!" and the horses sprang away from the ostlers' hands.

The leaders made good time. Past the old abbey and round and up the hill and away, soon leaving the stone houses clustered around the dominating castle far behind. Louise looked out. She caught a glimpse of Mr Jennings watching the coach. She put out her hand, holding her best lace handkerchief and waved. She saw his hand rise in return and then the coach turned a corner and they were on their way to York.

2

THE Black Bull at York proved even more impressive than the 'Royal George' at Richmond. Louise held back a little moan as she was helped out of the coach by a grinning ostler. It was late, and all Louise wanted was something hot to drink, a plate of steaming stew, preferably beef, and then bed.

The day's journey had been rough. Ruts, and rumours of highwaymen, had made the going slow. They had lurched through village after village, the relief driver blowing his horn and making a great commotion so that villagers and their children ran out to stare.

The first stop had been at Catterick Bridge, pulling in at the George Inn in great style. The delay had been only of a twenty minute duration but in that time, the whole of the Inn had been galvanized into action. Ostlers, porters, serving-wenches and pot-boys scurrying to do their job, and the landlord, a man with a fierce moustache and beard and wearing a snow-white apron over a corpulent stomach watching with a gimlet eye that all was as it should be.

His manners were good, and the ladies in the coach were all offered the facilities of the Inn, and a mug of hot, spiced ale. Two outside passengers alighted and there was an altercation regarding baggage. Finally, all was sorted out and on went the coach to the cheers of those left behind.

Louise only vaguely remembered passing through Northallerton and stopping to pick up a thin rusty figure dressed in black. He carried a brown leather bag, and the manner in which he clutched it to him he must have been carrying gold!

The man in black got out at Thirsk when the coach thundered to a stop at the Three Tuns, a large rather more modern Inn bustling with coming and going traffic. She was just in time to see the coach known as the North Briton leave the yard with a flurry of trumpetings. The ostlers springing back from the leaders heads, and the four-horse team eagerly leaping ahead. The horses were fresh and the brass sounding horn sent them forward like horses going into battle. Nostrils twitching, and foam already forming at their mouths, they lived only to pull the cumbersome coach.

The meal there, served quickly and efficiently, in the public room was taken with other passengers of other coaches. A leering passenger from the Leeds coach made Louise clutch Molly by the hand, and return to their own coach. They found the horses had been changed, and those who had not been able to afford a meal, already settled.

Inside the coach, they had a new passenger. A young lady, reeking of cheap violet scent and gin. She firmly squeezed herself into the best position and after the coach had left Thirsk, whiled away the time, talking to whoever was foolish enough to catch her eye.

Louise, uncomfortably placed in the middle of the coach saw very little of the passing scenery. The glimpses of verdant pasture-lands and fertile fields and wooded slopes, made her curse her new neighbour under her breath. It would have been nice to view the passing Yorkshire scene, maybe for the last time. Once in London, perhaps she would never be in a position to return!

So it was a tired and dispirited Louise who slept that night at the Black Bull with Molly beside her in a truckle-bed. At least the huge bed, with the feather mattress and thick feather quilt had been clean, even though the sheets had felt a little damp. There were no bed-bugs, but a mouse had disturbed her during the night.

The Black Bull was a noisy place, laughing and singing had gone on into the early hours, and at one point there was the sound of breaking glass and a woman's scream.

Louise shivered. This was all so different from what she had been used to. If all this happened in York, what would London be like? She slept uneasily, while Molly snored the night away.

The morning was cold and drizzly. Louise had bespoke breakfast in a private parlour. A huge log-fire burned merrily in the wide grate, and their table was set in an inglenook. Molly crouched low over the flames and admired the great log basket, already three or four inches deep in red ash.

"I wonder what time the maids are up in this place. Someone was stirring at four o'clock. I heard the great grandfather clock strike the hour."

"Perhaps the porters start early. Those logs would be too heavy for a girl."

"Hm, mebbe. But we're expected to lift loads nearly as big as ourselves."

"Well, there'll be no more heavy lifting for you, Molly. I'll see to that."

"Beggin' pardon, Miss. But what are we going to do in London?"

"Why, seek out my grandfather of course. He cannot refuse to give us shelter — at least until my affairs are sorted out. I will stress that I am not entirely penniless, even though my affairs will not be settled until I am twenty-five."

"But what if he is dead Miss! What then?" They stared at each other. Louise drew herself up but her lips quivered.

"That is a possibility I will not contemplate. I have given the matter some thought, and if my grandfather knew he was coming to the end of his life, I think he would have had some curiosity as to his grandchild. There would have been some communication, I don't doubt. No, I am persuaded he is still alive."

Molly sighed. Her round high-coloured face was unusually downcast.

"I 'opes so Miss. I'm afeared of London. Is it so very big? Much bigger than York? This place reminds me of an anthill — and the noise! Fair kept me awake all night."

"Nonsense, Molly. You slept like a baby."

"Oh Miss, I kept waking all night, truly I did!"

"Perhaps so, but you soon slept again!"

Breakfast over, Louise enquired about the London-bound post-chaise and booked a seat for them both inside. There would be a four hour delay before it was due out on its long journey. They would lie that night at Doncaster, after changing horses at Selby. There would be time to walk abroad in York and perhaps see the cathedral.

It was when they were ready to depart that Miss Kitty Marsden bumped into them. Miss Kitty of the violet scent and the outrageous scarlet and purple feathers. Now, the eye-catching hat was askew and the lady's bosom heaved in an unbecoming way.

"Oh my dears, how fortunate to meet again in this way." She gave a high giggle and strove to lessen her breathing. Her eyes darted behind them to the door of the public tap-room. "Are you bound for the London stage? We could walk together perhaps?"

Louise sighed inwardly and regarded the painted face before her. The shifty eyes looked from her to Molly, who seemed bemused at the lady's consequence. Before she could reply, the tap-room door burst open and a tall figure in a many-caped coat stormed out.

"Hey, you there! Stop. Come back!" But Miss Kitty darted away and round the corner of the inn-yard. Louise felt something fall near her foot. The stranger gave chase, and Louise had the impression of a huge dark man with angry blue eyes and a strong aggressive chin, as he dashed unceremoniously past.

The object near her foot was a purse. Molly gasped and picked it up giving it to Louise.

"Oh Miss, whatever next! That high-in-the-instep lady is nothing but a gabble-grinding hand-in-pocket shabrag!"

"Mm, so she is. It shows we are not up to snuff when we judge by a lady's finery. I wonder." She opened the purse, and

54

saw the glint of sovereigns. "This must be returned to that gentleman when he returns. There is no indication."

"Ha-ha, Madam, I've caught you in the act, have I?" The angry voice was just behind them. "Counting my money, to divide with your accomplice, I presume?" Louise turned round sharply.

"I-I beg your pardon?" She drew herself up in haughty disdain.

"Don't come your high horse with me! I know a straw damsel when I see one! You work in pairs. I know your sort. And is this poor girl in it too?" He looked at the staring Molly.

"I don't know what you mean! I found this purse."

"What a rapper! Do you take me for an addle-pot? Believe me, I am none such. I might drink in the tap-room, but I'm not wit-crackered. Pray pass over my money." He held out a long slim hand. Louise thrust the purse into it.

"Here, take it. I should have returned it to you in any case."

55

"You must think me a Charlie Chawbacon."

"Sir, you must think what you like. I am telling you the truth. My maid will bear me out. I think you are without conduct or delicacy, and whatever you say to the contrary, I think you are foxed!"

"Oho, the pretty little widgeon can set up her bristles! Believe me, Madam, I know the truth. You were in the act of counting those sovereigns. So don't try giving me a trimming. You are lucky that I am in a hurry to leave or I should have called the Runners!"

"How dare you speak so! It has gone beyond the bounds of all decency. I am no common thief. I'll have you know." He gripped her arm and swung her in front of him. The blue eyes blazed down into hers.

"I think you have more hair than wit! Do not cross me Madam. I have already told you I shall not call the Runners, but rouse my temper by your high-in-the-instep protestations and there is no knowing what I shall do!" He shoved her away, and turned on his heel, shouting for his coach.

It was a private coach, and Louise saw with some feeling that he was an accomplished whip and his matched bays in fine fettle. His coachman sat in stolid silence as the sleek light coach with the monogrammed panel charged out of the stable-yard, horses snorting and rearing, but held by a firm hand. She watched and hoped the coach would overturn somewhere along the road.

"Well! I've never heard the like!" Molly's eyes were starting out of their sockets. "To think anyone would think of you as a — a straw damsel! That's what he said, didn't he? Isn't that a name for a — ."

"That's enough, Molly. Forget what he said. He's nothing but a bosky upstart!"

"But he was a gentleman, Miss Louise. He spoke nice."

"He was as mifty as he was uncivil. I don't want to hear another word about him."

"Very well, Miss Louise. I only said — "

"That's enough. Not another word!" Molly relapsed into a sulky silence. Then she gave an exclamation.

"Lawks, here comes that flibberty fly-be-night! She looks up in the boughs about something."

Louise turned and watched Miss Kitty Marsden coming purposefully towards them.

"Oh my dears! What an experience. I was never so dumbstruck in my life. There he was, sat with chin on chest asleep before the tap-room fire — or so I thought. He should never have left his purse exposed in that fashion! It was not the work of a gentleman! I ask you, no honest person would leave a purse exposed in that circumstance. He *wanted* me to take it, I do declare!" She dabbed her eyes in a genteel manner. "I picked it up, what else could I do? It was asking to be taken? And then his hand shot out and if I had not been quick enough he would have had me. Oh yes, the monster was trying to trap me. I don't doubt to threaten and have his wicked way with me." Molly gasped.

"Ooo, we thought."

"Molly!" Louise's voice sounded a warning. Molly gulped and was silent. Kitty smiled and then looked from one to the other.

"Come on now, you're not as thick as winkle-pickers. Where's the blunt? I'll share even with you, and you can keep the purse."

"We haven't got it! We gave him it back."

"What? You gave? I see. You are roasting me. Want to keep the lot. I do the dangerous work and you take the dibs. Well you'll not diddle Flash Kitty! Come on now, pay up and we'll think naught of it."

"I tell you, he's got it. He accused me of being a-a straw damsel, whatever that is, and one of your partners. And I object most strongly."

Flash Kitty gave a great peel of laughter.

"You a straw damsel! You no more

look like one of them than I do a great lady. He must have been blind!" She wiped her eyes. "You know, I think you *are* telling the truth. It is a long time since I met such a birdwitted ninnyhammer. And you're going to London. Gawd help you!"

"I assure you we are, and I am not so goose-brained as you think. Also I really did give that man his money — or rather, he demanded it and took it."

"Ah, so you *were* going to keep it!" Her voice held a note of triumph.

"Not so. I had just determined to return it to him when he accused me."

She nodded her head and laughed again.

"Of being a straw damsel. And then?"

"Of receiving what you had stolen. I was much incensed, and when he demanded the purse I could not get rid of it fast enough."

"So! All my work for nothing! Ah well, for some reason I believe you. You've not the face of a flash! Come, we'll walk awhile. I have a mind to see what prospects there are for a girl like me."

"We were going to inspect the cathedral, and wander awhile along the great walls." Kitty made a move.

"Please yourself. It is not walls and cathedrals that I want to see. Good taverns and a place to do business, for me."

With a quick laugh over her shoulder, she picked up her skirts and trod carefully through the mud. Soon she was lost to sight in the narrow winding street. Louise and Molly walked close together, fearful of losing their way, but they found it an unpleasant experience, walking in York. The narrow streets, with overhanging houses, the danger of slops thrown from above and the interest shown from seedy-looking men on street corners made them give up the idea of going to the cathedral.

They found their way to the wider streets and gazed fascinated into the small shop windows, bow-fronted and glazed with small diamond panes. There were milliners, displaying plumed bonnets with reticules and gloves to match. Haberdashers, showing buttons and lace and ribbons, and the newest sets of collars and cuffs. Pastry-cooks offering wonderful confections and all manner of breads. Apothecaries, and their innumerable bottles and great glass jars of red and blue and purple liquid, and the grocers, butchers, candlemakers and the saddlers.

They were tired when they returned to the Black Bull with just twenty minutes to spare. A jug of small beer between them and a hot mutton pasty cheered them. And when the shouting and clamouring began outside, they knew the post-chaise was due.

It came in with a flourish, mud-splashed, and the tired horses flecked with foam, and steaming with sweat. Four ostlers sprang forward and Louise had never seen men work so fast. The four horses were uncoupled and four new blacks took their place, dancing and fresh and scenting the race ahead.

The new coach was brightly painted and bore the royal coat of arms. It proved lighter and better sprung, designed for long hard travelling distances.

This time Louise found herself in a corner seat with Molly beside her. She watched the porters bestowing the baggage in the basket behind, and a bulging mail-bag dumped unceremoniously between the driver and his guard. Serving wenches offering slopping tankards to eager outstretched hands, gawping children, narrowly missing the waiting horses plunging hooves, and muffin men and hot potato venders offering their wares and beggars getting in the way of the stable lads.

The landlord's stentorian tones brought a blush. He cursed and swore, and waved back the crowd.

"Give way, give way cullies. Another coach due in an hour. Damme Miss, are you for this coach? Get aboard Ma'am, if you intend travelling." Louise put out her head and beheld Kitty, panting and hot-cheeked and a porter carrying her bag. The door opened and Kitty sprawled inside, showing a lot of white-stockinged leg. There were whistles and catcalls and Louise turned her head away.

A fat woman opposite Louise sniffed, but a gentleman beside her smiled and moved away from the fat woman to make room.

"Henry, Sir," she boomed, "if you must make room for her, pray move this way. I am your wife and need your protection!"

"Not in the coach surely, Mildred my dear? It was easier for the lady, my removing farther, "he said mildly.

"Henry!" she said in an awful voice.

"Oh very well my dear. Can you step over my legs Ma'am?"

Kitty giggled, and made a face at the fat lady.

"Any time dear Sir. For you, I'll step over 'em, roll over em or sit on 'em." He gave a half-grin and then hastily turned it into a cough. The fat woman glared but apart from gripping her husband's hand tight, and moaning a little, made no answer.

"Are you unwell dear? In pain anywhere?" She smiled wanly.

"Only my old trouble. I think I am going to have a spasm."

"Oh dear, dear, and the coach has not even started yet!" She smiled with angelic patience.

"I am used to my affliction. I shall suffer with fortitude and put my trust in God. Did you remember the gin?"

"Yes my love, if the pain gets too bad, I have it ready."

"Good, good. I know you will watch over me, good husband that you are."

"There, there now. Close your eyes and rest awhile." She wriggled.

"If only we had more room." She glared at Kitty and then leant back, belching audibly. "I think that pork was a little too fat. What do you think Henry? HENRY." But Henry was now smiling at Kitty who had settled herself beside him.

"Yes, yes dear, as you say, are you

comfortable Ma'am?" Kitty smiled impishly at him, and her hand crept to his, which seemed to disappear under the folds of her skirt.

Louise was shocked. More shocked than she'd ever been in her life, and she did not know where to look! The possibility of contemplating a flirtation in a coach and under the nose of an ailing wife was well past the bounds of good conduct and delicacy. Miss Kitty Marsden was a person of a kind she had never met before. She watched her like some new specie.

She was intrigued and fascinated and horrified, but the effect on the other gentlemen in the coach made her reflect. Each man watched closely and Louise recognized the hot light in their eyes. One man never took his eyes off her ankles, and Louise saw her smile at him and lift her skirt another inch.

Then the postillion gave a resounding blast, the signal for departure, and the ostlers sprang away from the horses heads and they began the long haul ahead. There would be a stop at Selby for food and a change of horses, and then no more until they reached Doncaster.

The time passed slowly, Louise watching the changing scenery with interest, noting the stone walls giving way to neat hedges and smaller fields and less open moor. Villages were often a long straggle of houses, mostly with their own garden, a church with tall grey spire showing above a spread of trees and perhaps one or two alehouses, not big enough to stop at. Occasionally there was the glimpse of a manor-house or a greater pile, a castle perhaps? Louise wondered and would have liked to stop and explore. Molly and the fat woman slept part of the time, the fat woman complaining about a queasiness of spirit and having frequent doses of medicinal gin. Her subsequent gin-laden breath combining with Kitty's violet scent and the body odour in the close atmosphere of the coach made the journey seem endless.

At last they arrived in Doncaster, and found a comfortable bed awaiting them both. That night Louise slept right through the drunken midnight revels of certain city gentlemen.

And that was the pattern of the journey. A night at the Rose and Crown in Tonbridge, and on again. Changes of horses, a long haul and a welcome at the White Horse at Socon, a change of passengers, and a night at the Roebuck at Knebworth. Kitty and the fat woman kept a kind of battle going for the erring husband's interest. Kitty winning hands down. She had even confided to Louise while they were at the White Horse that dear Mr Jepson wanted to meet her in London and had suggested a trysting place!

At last the post-chaise and galloping horses arrived with a flourish into the Angel yard in Islington, only an hour and ten minutes late, which was a great achievement. The journey was over, and Louise sighed with relief.

Gathering their belongings together, they stopped only long enough to ask directions to Wood Lane in Cheapside.

The porter who they asked, laughed.

"Cheapside? 'Tis a long way from here. You'll not get a chair tonight to Cheapside. Best wait until morning. Go along that street until you come to the sign of the Fighting Cock and knock at the house next door. Tell them that Joe sent you. You'll be comfortable there."

"Thank you. Here's twopence for your pains."

"Thank you Ma'am. You'll find no bugs there. It is a clean house, rough, but they're honest — after a fashion."

Joe proved right. The food was plain but well enough cooked. The ale tolerable and the beds hard but clean.

The sun shone next morning, throwing into strong relief the close-built grimy houses, the dirty windows and the garbage. Strong smells wafted up from the gutters, reminding Louise of the middens at home, but these smells were not of cattle and pigs.

At first they walked, but again Joe was right. They had no idea where Cheapside was. They could be walking away from it. A passing drayman whistled to Molly. She smiled and waved.

"Where are you bound?" he bawled.

"Cheapside."

"Would you like a ride? I'm going so far that way." He pulled up, his great bay carthorse bringing sparks on the cobbles. Molly flung up the bundles and Louise gripping her carpet-bag followed her. They sat down beside him and with a jerk of the reins they were away.

For a while the man sat smoking quietly. The smell of his strong tobacco made Louise want to cough, but a ride was better than walking through all the streets assorted filth. Then his eyes slid over them.

"What's two young ladies doing out alone around here? Don't you know it's dangerous?" Louise coughed.

"We came in on the stage last night. We have come to London from Yorkshire."

"I thought by your complexions you were from the country. I'm from Hampshire myself."

"We are going to Mr Tyndal residing

70

in Wood Lane, draper and merchant. Have you heard of him?"

"Tyndal? Tyndal? No. There's lots of shops in Cheapside. Are you going as servants to this Mr Tyndal?"

"No. I'm his granddaughter, and Molly is my maid."

"Oh, then I'd best take you there. There'll be money in it perhaps?"

"Oh I can pay you, never fear."

"Half a sovereign perhaps?"

"What? Five shillings. No more."

"Very well. Five shillings it is. You're not such a green goose as you look!"

"Thank you. I may be unversed in London ways, but I am no ninnyhammer to be fleeced by every Jonny-cum-Piccolo!"

"Oh, come now Ma'am, I only — "

"I know. You thought I was a birdwitted puddinghead, frightened into paying double. I am not frightened and I assure you I am not a fool."

The rest of the journey was made in silence. Then the dray pulled up in a narrow street in front of a shabby shop needing a new coat of paint. The windows were cobwebbed and Louise pursed her lips. Her grandfather evidently needed help!

The drayman handed down the baggage and Molly stood while Louise fumbled for the five shillings.

"Thank you. Here is the five shillings, even though I think you took the long way round. I am sure we passed the same street twice. I observed the Inn sign which depicted a black swan. Never mind, we are here."

"Thank you Ma'am. I'll be on my way." The man sounded flustered and he jerked his reins and the lumbering horse moved away.

While they stood surveying the shop and Louise mastered the sudden emotion inside her, a crowd of ragged children gathered around. One poked Molly and giggled. She swung round, and slapped his face.

"'ere, you show more respect! Get back all of you, or we'll whistle up the Bow Street Runners!"

A general laugh went up.

"Garn!" The leading tormentor jeered. "The Runners keep away from these parts. Too many narks and sheenies round 'ere. Who you want?"

"Never you mind. Run away you cheeky little devil." Molly picked up the bundles. "Well Miss, we'd better make ourselves known."

"Oh Molly, do you think we did right?"

"That I can't say Miss, but we'll soon find out!"

They opened the door of the shop and a rusty bell overhead tinkled. Inside, the atmosphere smelt fusty. The shelves of the shop were crammed higgledy-piggledy with all manner of goods. Candlesticks, pewter mugs, cockaded hats, a sword, articles of clothing, a number of fans, watches and a carriage-lamp and an endless variety of household utensils, chamber-pots not being the least of them.

The shop was dim, for very little light came through the grimy window. Louise started nervously when an old dirty figure shuffled through a door leading to another inner pool of blackness.

"Yes?" The old shrewd eyes travelled over the neat pellise and heavy travelling skirt peeping underneath. They gleamed, and his mittened fingers pulled at his sparse grey beard. "What can I do for a young Miss like you? Do you wish to pawn something? Or is it a loan you seek?" He leered. "Or are you in trouble? Is it the abortionist you want? Speak. There need be no dissembling here."

"I-I, it is none of these things. Are you Josiah Tyndal?"

The cunning eyes narrowed.

"Who wants to know?"

"I am his granddaughter."

"His granddaughter. Josiah's granddaughter! Well, well, well!"

Louise felt a sudden relief. Her stomach had tightened at the thought of this smelly old man being her grandfather.

"I take it you are not my grandfather?"

"Nay lass. Having never being married, I've neither chick nor child, but Josiah Tyndal does not live here any more. I bought his business and he moved nearer to Mayfair, oh, four or is it five years ago? For all I know he may be dead. Granddaughter! Well, well, well! A close man, old Josiah. Never once mentioned a granddaughter." He laughed a wheezy throaty laugh. "If you want lodgings, I'm not above taking two pretty girls in. What d'ye say?" He licked his lips and his yellowed hands with the long dirty nails gave a convulsive clutching movement. Louise grabbed the bemused Molly and dragged her to the door.

"No, thank you. Come on Molly, let us get out into the fresh air." Pushing and shoving, Louise got Molly outside. Then half-running they went back the way the dray had brought them.

"Hey, come back!" Louise glanced behind her. The old man was waving at them. "Don't you want to know where Josiah Tyndal lives? A guinea for his situation!"

But Louise only sobbed and ran on. Panic held sway and for the first time wondered whether George Holdsworth would have been a better fate. They turned a corner into a busier thoroughfare and walked some way before Louise could control her tears. Molly thoroughly alarmed at the way her strong-minded young mistress had broken down cried too. They were lost and friendless among the seething mass of Londoners who were all ready to rend and tear.

A curricle drawn by two matched greys came tearing around a corner catching Louise and Molly unawares. People scattered and a young boy carrying a basket of salted herrings on his head, leapt into a doorway. The flying hooves nearly caught Louise and she stumbled over the cobbles going full length into the mud and ooze underfoot. Molly screamed, and the young dandy in the curricle pulled up in such a hurry, his horses reared on to their haunches and pawed the air.

Molly let fly a string of invective, indignantly aware of the undignified presence of her mistress. Louise lay where she had fallen, one hand clutching a handful of mud and the other, her now wet and sticky carpet-bag. A ragged youth grabbed the left-hand horse's bit. The young man leapt down and soothing and gentling the horses first, he motioned another interested spectator to hold the other's head.

Then mincing forward he held out a languid hand to Louise.

"Allow me, Ma'am. My most humble apologies Ma'am, for the predicament you are in."

Louise stared up at the apparition in plum coat and high neckcloth and the whitest pantaloons she had ever seen. His glossy hessians with the gold tassels were now sadly muddied. He sighed at the sight of them, but manfully hid his chagrin. He swept off his hat revealing a head of well ordered blond curls. He was young, not much older than she herself. He smiled and she smiled back.

"Come now, take my hand and rise." Reluctantly Louise allowed herself to be raised to her feet.

"Thank you," she muttered, too

flustered and vexed with herself for falling in that silly manner, to show good manners.

"Allow me to present myself, Roland Theobold, at your service."

"How do you do Mr Theobold? I am Miss Belgower, lately from Yorkshire."

"May I take you somewhere, Miss Belgower? Surely, in your present state?" He looked meaningly at her muddied appearance.

"Alas, we have nowhere to go at the present moment. We are without lodging."

"Then I must take you to Brook Street where I reside. Your maid will make sure the proprieties are kept. 'Twas my fault you are in the state you are. I must rectify my fault."

"But — "

"Please, may I hand you both up? This locality is not conducive to polite conversation. We will repair to my lodging forthwith."

Masterfully, he had his way and Louise thankfully sat down on the high seat of the curricle with Molly squashed in beside her. Nothing more was said until they stopped and a groom ran out of the side opening to the house in Brook Street. The curricle was driven away and Mr Theobold led the way inside.

An intrigued butler coughed, and led the way to the withdrawing room. He looked down his nose at Molly, but as Mr Theobold gave no instructions about the maid, she was allowed to enter the with-drawing room.

Louise got a vague impression of a blue and gold room, not too large but opulent, with several good pictures and several marble statues and many overstuffed cushions on couches and chairs, and fine ornaments on whatnots and the overmantel. A good fire burned however, and it was comfortable.

"My mother's taste, not my brother's — or mine," he said hastily.

"Oh, it is not a lodging in the broadest sense of the word?"

"No Ma'am. I lodge here when in Town, but it is my brother's house. We have an arrangement."

"Very convenient, and amicable of him, I am sure!"

"Yes. He is a good brother, mayhap a little stern. He is much older than I, and most forgot how a fellow flies high with his bosom companions!"

"Then perhaps we should not be here. He will not like this intrusion."

"Make yourself easy Ma'am. He would but give me a trimming for driving his cattle too hard. He cares for his cattle more than he does for me!" He grinned, and so, belying the exaggeration. "Ah here comes Bexton with tea. You will take tea before you renew your toilet?"

"Renew my toilet? But — "

"I have given orders for water to be heated. You cannot go forth soiled and bedraggled! Consider, what a scandal-broth it could turn out to be. Besides I should not be so rag-mannered as to allow you to. The housekeeper will clean your pelisse and everything will be most respectable, I assure you."

"Then you are very kind Sir. And I

will be pleased to avail myself of your offer."

"Good. Now drink your tea and then a meal will be prepared for you later."

A young servant in lace mob-cap and grey-striped dress — very prim, and covered by a snowy-white apron conducted them up to a large rather masculine bedroom. A fire burned in the grate and a hip-bath held steaming hot water and several pristine towels were laid hard by. Scented soap was in a holder near by for Molly to hand to her.

Somehow, the room did not match with young Mr Theobold, but it was comfortable and rich in a subdued kind of way. She had imagined his taste would run to gold cupids and silken curtains of bright clear hues. But perhaps, the gold and dull green brocade was his mother's taste too.

She enjoyed the bath. The water was surprisingly clear for London. She had understood there was much pollution in London wells and many people preferred water from the River Thames. Molly handed her a large towel in which she enveloped herself. Molly quickly washing and taking the advantage to change herself. Louise shook out her hair and dried it near the fire.

"Take your time Molly. We may as well make the most of this." Gently she combed out the tangles in her hair and the heat from the fire made her a little drowsy.

"Miss, if it's all right with you, I'll look in this cupboard. I think it could be a powder-room. There might also be cleaning materials for boots and shoes. Our shoes are a sight!"

"Yes, do so, or we shall leave a trail of mud behind that the housekeeper will take umbrage to."

Molly stepped inside, and the door swung to. Louise hummed a little tune. She was feeling in spirits once again. It was marvellous how a bath and clean linen could lift up morale!

There was the sound of the outer door opening and a smothered curse. Louise turned her head sharply, and froze where she crouched. The towel fell unheeded around her, showing smooth rounded shoulders that glistened and the hint of bare cleavage. The stranger took all that in in one glance, before a hot tide of colour suffused her face and she made a grab for the falling towel.

"The straw damsel! What in the world are you doing here? One of Roland's bits of muslin, I expect, but I never thought he would go so far as to introduce one to my bedchamber!"

He stood over her, overpoweringly dark and menacing. His smile, both disdainful and insulting. Surprise and shock paralysed her brain.

"You!" She recognized the very unpleasant man she had encountered in York. "What are you doing here? Have you been following me?" she stuttered stupidly.

"No Ma'am, you flatter yourself. I live here. I am Lord Falconer, and I ask, nay command, you to leave my house at your very earliest convenience!"

3

THE door slammed behind him. Louise could only stare at where he had been standing. That was the second time he had called her a straw damsel and inferred — she clenched her fists. Uncontrolled anger welled up inside her until she shook.

Molly coming out of the cupboard wide-eyed said, "Lor, Miss, what was all the commotion? It sounded like Farmer Joplin's bull, it did."

"Mr Theobold's brother, I presume." Louise said tightly. "We have our orders to leave forthwith. So much for Mr Theobold's assurances that everything was in order. Come, help me into my shift and my stays."

"Oooh, did he see you just in the towel?" She started to giggle.

"Molly, that is more than enough. You show a want of delicacy. Come, pass me those clean petticoats and bundle the soiled clothes into my bag. We must leave at once."

"Will you wear the blue merino Miss?" Molly's voice was subdued. She knew she had taken advantage of the free and easy situation between them. Sometimes it had been hard to remember that Miss Louise was indeed her mistress.

"Yes, and do go and find the housekeeper and bring back my pellise, cleaned or no. I want to leave, forthwith."

"Yes Miss." Molly knew authority when she heard it, and Louise at the moment was at her most belligerent.

She came back with it and with her, the housekeeper.

"I am sore Miss. I have not made a thorough job of it. The mud you know."

"Thank you, you have done wonders in the time. Pray take this." She held out a florin. The woman drew herself up.

"Indeed Ma'am, I could not. I only obey orders from the young master. Thank you Ma'am."

"Then thank you. Now, I think we

should leave. Please convey our thanks to Mr Theobold, and our excuses. We must be on our way."

"But he is waiting downstairs in the dining-room. I have ordered a cold collation for you. Cook will be upset."

"I am sorry. We must go. Thank Cook for me and assure her, it is of the most importance that we go now."

"Very well. But what of Mr Roland Ma'am, what shall I say to him?"

"Tell him to refer himself to his brother. He will understand."

"Very well, Ma'am."

She led the way downstairs, and spoke quietly to the butler hovering in the hall. He looked startled, and then bowed to Louise and hastened to open the door.

They were down the steps and walking away with the bundles and bag when the door burst open and Mr Theobold catapulted himself down the steps of the imposing Brook Street house.

"Hey! Where are you going? I don't understand. Why do you run away without a word to me?" Louise stopped and turned to face him.

"Ask your brother," she said brusquely. "Have you not seen him?"

"Why yes, for a moment or two. He came home unexpectedly. I think he is in the book-room. Why?"

"Did he not tell you, he surprised me in his bedchamber?"

"His bedchamber?" Roland stared at her, and then started to laugh. "No. I thought he had gone straight into his book-room. He caught you?"

"I'm afraid I do not share your merriment. I was all but undone and he accused me of — of — ."

"Of what pray?" Now young Mr Theobold's face had gone white and cold. "Damme answer, will you? What did he accuse you of."

"I would rather not say, but he was most uncivil and offensive."

"Oh he was, was he?" Mr Theobold spoke through clenched teeth.

"By George! I'll draw his claret! I'll give him a leveller that he'll not forget for a while! Of all the mutton-headed cockle-brained — ”

“Would you be by any chance talking about me?” The cool amused voice stopped Mr Theobold in full flow. Louise looked up at the hated figure standing gracefully on the top step. He had shed his caped coat and appeared slimmer and more graceful. Dressed in an exquisitely cut blue stuff coat with a brocade waistcoat over a ruffled shirt, and buff pantaloons and glossy hessians, he appeared more swarthy against the froth of well tied cravat. Mr Theobold blushed.

“Damme, Marcus. What is this about you insulting the lady? She means to run away without partaking of the luncheon I bespoke for her.”

“Perhaps she feels out of place.”

“Out of place? Are you mad?” They glared at each other.

“Are you? Just why do you bring one of your frail barques here, to my house? Is she so special?”

“Frail Barque?” Mr Theobold spluttered. “Are you suggesting?”

"Pray, come in off the street, all of you. We cannot have an altercation out in the open. The next thing, it will be the latest on-dit. You would like that, I suppose?" turning to Louise. "It would give you a certain notoriety, would it not? To be the subject of argument between brothers."

There was a scuffle and Lord Falconer reeled back with a blooded nose. Crimson dripped down on to his exquisite cravat. He held a lace handkerchief to his nose and wiped the blood.

"So the little lady holds your affections! I am sorry but you will have to remove to other lodgings where you can carry on your love idyll. I'll have none of it here. And while you are about it, watch your purse! She's quite an expert!"

So now he was insisting on her being a thief too! Louise took a deep breath, and stepped forward.

"You are disgusting! Of all the conceited, self-opinionated rag-mannered stubborn persons I have known, you beat the lot." She paused to take breath.

He grinned crookedly, his nose was now swelling.

"Watch out, she's mad enough to tie her garter in public!" Both Molly and Mr Theobold winced as Louise's hand cracked across the grinning face. His eyes narrowed.

"Nobody does that to me, and gets away with it!" Before she was aware of his intentions, he picked her up in his arms and ran lightly up the steps and into the house.

"Put me down," she yelled, "or I'll call the Runners!" Her hands beat in vain on his chest. Molly and Mr Theobold ran up the steps behind them.

"Oh Miss, are you all right?" Molly was ready for both murder and rape. She swung one of the bundles and caught Lord Falconer on the side of the head. It opened and a cascade of small clothes scattered over the floor.

"Molly!" screamed Louise, "What have you done? Pick them up this instance."

"Why the hysterics Ma'am? Surely you are used to having your smalls ogled?"

He put her down gently, but held on to her arm. "Now into the dining-room if you please."

"I have told you until I am quite sick. I am no trollop, which I understand you are accusing me of. I am not a light-fingered flash as a certain lady we both know, would say, and I am not contemplating an alliance with your brother. So now, can my maid and myself go?"

"I think you have forgotten I found you en déshabillé? It is not customary for a lady to visit a gentleman in his lodging, even if it is his brother's house. And certainly not to stop and take a bath! Most improper." He shrugged. "You must see, what else can I think? Especially after York!"

Louise lost her temper and stamped her foot.

"My Lord, did you enquire as to my visit here? Have you once asked for an explanation? Do you not think there could be some good reason for all this — this!"

"Unconventional circumstance?"

"Well, yes." She bit her lip. He smiled grimly.

"A gentleman does not ask questions. He looks at a situation as it is and draws his own conclusions. One does not question a lady's motives!"

"Oh! You make it all sound so questionable. You are most uncivil and overbearing." She turned her back on him, unable to hide her tears. She sniffed audibly. A hand waved a lace handkerchief before her eyes.

"Here, use this. I cannot abide snuffling. Tears, yes, but snuffling is for the lower classes."

"You are insufferable," but she took the handkerchief and blew, secretly pleased to spoil the pristine freshness. She handed it back.

"Keep it. It will remind you of the day you cried in temper in public! Now, Roland will be wondering what kept us both. I should think he will have finished his luncheon. He has a healthy appetite, that young man." Gently, but inexorably, he led her to the dining parlour where Roland was already seated, eating and brooding. He cast a look of dislike at his brother.

"Ah, so you prevailed on Miss Belgower to partake of luncheon. Come, make yourself comfortable. Bexton here will take Molly below and see that she is fed." He patted the richly brocaded seat beside him. "Do you eat with us Marcus?"

"No. I have business to attend to. About that blow, I shall speak with you later. Miss Belgower, your servant." He bowed mockingly, and moved to the door. "Oh, and Roland, that was a good blow, firm and true, but a little off centre. You should take some lessons from Gentleman Jackson. I shall introduce you to him!" The door closed behind him. Young Mr Theobold glowered.

"He always manages to make me feel in the wrong. I'll better him one of these days," he growled. "He's always so right. He disapproves of me. Doesn't like my dress, my friends or my habits."

He sighed. "More like a father than a brother!"

"Perhaps he is just an ill-mannered boor, and cannot help himself. I consider him a vulgar-minded rake-shame!"

"Oh, Ma'am, I think that is a little strong. Try the beef and pickles. Cook's noted for her pottage. No, to be fair, Marcus is no rake-shame. A prosy fellow, but no hell-firing psalm-singer. One of the best really, but so damnably right. Begging your pardon Ma'am."

"Well he is vulgar-minded — to think as he did. Hm, the beef is good. Lord Falconer must be congratulated on his cook. As I was saying, he was quick in his conclusions."

"My fault. I should have spoken with him, and apprised him of the situation."

"Then why did you not? It would have become you as a gentleman."

Mr Theobold looked uncomfortable. His face reddened.

"The horses, I was not supposed — "

"You had not permission to take them out?" She stared at him in amazement.

"You are actually frightened of Lord Falconer?"

"Well, he can be quite formidable on occasion. He could send me on a repairing lease to our country estate. I do not want that to happen."

"So you preferred to let him think what he did, rather than the truth." Louise was indignant and showed it.

"How was I to know he would get on his high horse?"

"Might I remind you it was my reputation at stake?"

"I did not think."

"Now I quite understand your brother being always right. You are very young, are you not?" He moved uncomfortably.

"I am older than you. Now I think it is you who are uncivil. I could have driven on and left you lying in the mud." They glared at each other like brother and sister. Then Mr Theobold dropped his eyes. "Here, try some of Cook's egg-custard spiced with nutmegs, or the scalded cream. Both good and to be recommended."

"Thank you, a little custard if you please." They ate in silence.

They were sipping their coffee when Mr Theobold suddenly had a brainwave.

"You have no lodging! We must find a place for you to stay. Do you know anyone in London? Can I take you anywhere?"

"Alas, I came to find my grandfather, but he has removed from his place of sojourn."

"Could we not find out where he lives?"

"I do not know how to set about it. There are so many people here in London. It could be difficult."

"Nonsense! If he is of consequence someone will know of him. What is his name?"

"I do not think you will have heard of him. He was in trade. A draper and mercer to be exact."

"Oh, I thought — " His fair face blushed again, and he looked uncomfortable. He mumbled and then stopped.

"You thought I was of the quality?"

Her lips curled. "I'm sorry to be so disappointing. My grandfather is one, Josiah Tyndal. Does he mean anything to you? I doubt it." She turned away and used her finger-bowl and so missed his look of acute embarrassment.

He was silent so long, she looked up in curiosity.

"Is anything wrong? You look a little pale."

"Anything wrong? No. Why should there be?" His voice sounded defiant.

"I don't know. You seem a little strange. Do you know my grandfather?"

"No. I don't. At least, I think I've heard the name. If it is the same man, he lives in Boss Lane just off Mayfair."

"Mayfair! The horrible man in the shop mentioned Mayfair. It could be he! Oh, how wonderful. You can take me there." Louise was all smiles, not noticing Mr Theobold's uncomfortable silence. Then his thoughts overcame him.

"You can't possibly be related to that

revolting old man?" he burst out, and then stopped.

Louise froze. Suddenly the welcome news was not quite so welcome.

"Why? What do you mean? I thought you did not know him." They stared at each other and Mr Theobold moved uneasily.

"I don't. Well I mean, that is, I've done business with him. I don't know him socially." He ended on a rush.

"Business? What business have you had with him? Surely you are too young to do business with anyone?"

"I beg your pardon. I am turned twenty! I'm no halfling, you know." He sounded hurt. "If you want to know," and now there was a hint of malice in his tone. "He is a percenter!" At her look of bewilderment he went on, "A Jewboy, but not a Jew. Gad! You still do not understand! A money-lender! And a wizard to boot!"

"A money-lender!" Louise's eyes opened wide.

"Yes, and a damned shrewd one at

that! His rates are cheaper than the Jews, but he's just as ruthless."

"And you've had dealings with him You've actually borrowed money from him?" Louise sounded scandalized.

"Well yes, if he's the same man. There is nothing wrong in that! All my friends and acquaintances go to him. He's better than the Jews!"

"But what about your brother? Does he not disapprove?"

"Of course he disapproves! Old Tyndal is one of the main reasons we don't see eye to eye! He thinks I should live within my allowance. I can't touch my own money for ten months. He's a regular clutch-fisted nip-shot with me. He's forgotten that a Town Buck needs plenty of blunt to cut a decent figure!"

"And you call it cutting a decent figure to spend money wildly. Money not even your own? And my grandfather encourages you?" She said this bitterly. This relative was so very different to her dear Papa!

"Well, it is Marcus' fault. He should

allow for gaming debts. He introduced me to White's and Gunn's, and Pegg's Coffee-Shoppe. A gentleman cannot walk out of a game when he starts losing. And if he is winning, he must stay to give the other fellows their chance of revenge. It is only becoming to a gentleman!"

"I don't understand it. You talk of honour, and yet you gamble away someone else's money!"

"But once borrowed it becomes my money, and I can do what I like with that!"

"But what about repayments? And the interest?"

"Old Tyndal knows we're all up to snuff. He'll get his money, there's no risk. It is only a matter of me coming of age, and thirty percent is not too bad. A bargain really. Old Reuben Bernstein charges fifty-five per cent. So old Tyndal's rates are a bargain. Not to be sniffed at!"

"I think it is all highly irregular. I am ashamed my grandfather has resorted to this kind of living. Better an honest shopkeeper."

"A shopkeeper does not make the money, and does not take the risk."

"You said there was no risk!"

"Not with me. But some of his clients get in so deep, that there is only suicide left or they choose duelling as their way out. I've known many a hot-headed youth deliberately pick a quarrel to save his family from dishonour, and died with a smile on his lips. The money-lenders do not advertize their involvement with the reason for sudden death."

"It is monstrous and should be stopped."

"Do not confide your ideas to your grandfather. He may not appreciate your concern."

"I think perhaps I should make my way there with all speed. If you would be so good as to call me a cab?"

"Nay, I shall take you myself. Marcus left orders to use the town coach at my discretion in your service."

"Very thoughtful of him, I'm sure!" Louise felt that she should have appreciated the offer more, but perversely she hated the idea of being beholden to such a detestable man!

The journey from Brook Street did not take long. Molly was inclined to talk. She was excited by the large kitchen in Brook Street and the wonderful array of brass and copper pans and kitchen aids.

"And they have a wonderful contraption that turns the spit over the fire. It is a cage, with pulleys and Cook's small dog runs inside a wheel, thereby turning the great joint slung over the fire! An improvement to a small boy turning a handle!"

"Perhaps, but losing some small boy from a job! Think of that. If all the jobs were made easy, someone is bound to suffer. There are always too few jobs for too many persons."

"I never thought of that." Molly relapsed into silence, to re-think the situation with the job.

"It must be cheaper to employ a dog instead of a boy. The dog has taken the boy's job. I see what you mean . . . "

The coach stopped outside a tall narrow building, with well-worn steps running up to a stout oak door. Molly raised her eyes at the state of the steps.

"Never seen soap and water or scouring stone for months!" said Molly contemptuously. "The windows are dirty too. What kind of servants are these who do not look to the outer appearance of the house? And look at those stout shutters! Fastened, the house could withstand a siege!"

Mr Theobold heard her, and grinned at Louise.

"The percenters need shutters. Protect them from angry clients and the hungry mob. We get rioters in the city every so often. Hunger marchers, dissenters and protesters against George and his ever-mounting debts. The Prince of Wales has much to answer for."

"He shows no example to his fellow men. My Papa had very pronounced views on the Prince of Wales!"

"He gives a large amount of work to the poor people however."

"Very nice when they get paid!" Her tone was acid.

Mr Theobold laughed. He looked up at the tall house.

"No good will come of sitting here and arguing. Jem will walk the horses up and down until I get you installed. I'll just knock first and make sure someone is at home." He leapt lightly down and ran up the steps, pulling an old bell-handle. For a long while nothing happened.

Louise sat, craning her neck watching for the door to open. Her heart bumped. She was nervous and now when there was to be a confrontation, apprehensive of the outcome. Would he welcome her?

At last the door creaked back as if not often used. A wrinkled face topped by a grimy mob-cap looked out.

"If it's business, go round the back," she snapped and started to close the door, but Mr Theobold was quick. One polished hessian boot stuck firmly in the way.

"Hey, not so fast. Is Mr Tyndal at home?"

"Yes, haven't I just told you to go round the back? His business is conducted at the back." She nodded in the direction of a side door.

"My good woman we are not here on that kind of business! Tell your master that Miss Belgower is here to see him."

"Who?" The woman's small black eyes peered past Mr Theobold at the coach.

"Miss Belgower."

"Never heard of her, and I've worked for him this past fifteen years. Are you at the right house?"

"It is none of your business. Just do as I say and go to Mr Tyndal with the message."

"He's busy with a client. You'll have to wait."

"Very well. I'll bring the lady inside and her baggage."

"Her baggage? Oh, the master will not like that! We never has visitors to stay. I shouldn't bring the baggage in. You'll only have to take it out again!"

"We must take a chance on that." He waved to Louise and then ran down to the coach, handing Louise and then Molly down.

"The old woman's a bit of a dragon," he whispered. "Not keen on your staying. Your grandfather is with a client. I wonder who it is?" The bundles and carpet-bag were soon bestowed in the dark front hall of the house.

The old woman showed them into a musty smelling front parlour and pulled back the heavy draped curtains. It was dusty and showed little signs of usage.

"You can sit there," she muttered and after giving Molly a glare walked out and slammed the door.

Louise looked around. It was not as she expected. The dark oak panelling, the worn carpet with little pattern left and the lumpy horsehair furniture made it a chill, inelegant room. Her eyes gave mute appeal to Mr Theobold. He shifted uneasily under her gaze.

"It might be better than you think. You are not in queer stirrups yet." He moved to the window to hide his concern for her. He noted the affluent houses on the other side. So old Fox Tyndal lived this way because he wanted to! Probably would rather make money than spend it. In other words, a clutch-fisted miser! He was ruminating on the fate of Louise when he espied the side door open and a furtive figure come out and look both ways.

"By George!" he said excitedly, "that's Monkey Gainsbrough down there. I always thought he was full of juice. Well, well, well. You can never tell these days can you?"

Louise started nervously. She had gone very white.

"Who? Do you know him well?"

"Fairly well. Took a monkey off me the other night. That's why he's called Monkey. Stops gambling then and walks away. Doesn't give a fellow a chance. And yet he has to come here. Strange, are you not well Ma'am? You look very pale."

"It is just this waiting, and this dreadful room. I feel a blackness of the spirits come over me."

"I'm not surprised. Gloomy place. Are

you sure you want to stay? Come home with me. Marcus isn't a bad chap really. He'll put you up."

"I would not dream of it! I should not like to be beholden to him. Better this than his gibes and innuendoes."

"I think when he knows you better there would be no more innuendoes. He spoke in ignorance."

"All the more reason for giving me the benefit of the doubt! Please let us not talk about him. How much longer do you think we shall have to wait?"

"Not long. I think I can hear someone now."

He was right. The old woman came back into the room. Now, she showed more interest in Louise.

"Will you come this way Miss? And you too, Sir? Master will see you now." She led the way down a long dark corridor to the back of the house. A smell of stale cooking came up from a cellar stairway. She knocked and then opened a dark brown painted door.

"His place of business," whispered

Mr Theobold, who recognized his surroundings. Louise nodded and entered the room.

At first she saw no one. There were several chairs upholstered in grimy brocade and a huge desk with several quills standing in a jar. Then as her eyes adjusted themselves to the dimness of the room, she saw the movement of a small man seated behind the desk.

Mr Theobold coughed and spoke diffidently.

"Mr Tyndal Sir, I have brought you Miss Belgower, your granddaughter. I found her in desperate circumstances, and already knowing you, I brought her here."

"Eh? Whats that you say? My granddaughter? Impossible. I have no granddaughter. Do you take me for a fool, young man?"

"No Sir. Not at all Sir." He looked from Louise to the old man. "She told me she was your granddaughter." His voice tailed away.

"Come nearer young man. Let me see

who it is." The little man stood up, peering through steel-rimmed spectacles. A maroon smoking cap on his head threatened to slip off. He adjusted it. "Hm, young Theobold is it? I have just written to you today. Have you brought me the amount due?"

"No Sir. I have not received your letter yet, Sir."

"Strange. I sent it by hand. That boy Thomas, is a lazy sot. Will have words with him when he returns. Now about the wench. Tell me about her."

Louise pushed Mr Theobold aside.

"I can speak for myself." Her voice sounded firmer than she really was. "You are Mr Josiah Tyndal, late of Wood Lane, draper and mercer?"

"Yes, what of it? Everyone knows that." The old rheumy eyes looked her up and down.

"You had a daughter, Almira?"

"Yes, yes, but she has not been spoken of for nearly twenty years."

"I am her daughter, Louise."

"I have no grandchild! Go back where

you came from. I want naught to do with you. How do I know you speak the truth?" He held his head on one side and looked slyly over the rims of his spectacles.

"I have papers and letters from you to my mother."

"How do I know that you have not found them somewhere and are trying to fob yourself off as my granddaughter?"

"Take a look at me, Mr Tyndal. Do you not see anything of my mother in me?" The old man came round from behind the desk and motioned her to the light of the grimy window.

"Come here where I can see you better." For a long moment he stared at her, then he nodded his head slowly. "You could be, I'm not saying you are mind!" he said sharply. "You could be after my money." He fingered his stubbly chin and the rasp of it set Louise's teeth on edge.

"I assure you that is not the case. I was not aware you had money. I have a letter from Mr Jennings, my father's

111

solicitor. Would you read it?"

"Mr Jennings, hey? What of your father?"

"He is dead. Otherwise I should not be here."

"Ah, so you admit making use of me! Give me the letter."

"I only ask for your protection. Grandfather . . . may I call you so? I am in sorry straits."

"Be quiet while I read this letter."

There was silence a long while after he finished. Then he sighed and laid down the letter.

"Almira was always a fool, and so was your father. I never forgave him for shillyshallying. He must needs meet my daughter in secret rather than ask me, man to man for permission to address her. And you know why? Because she was a shopkeeper's daughter. He was ashamed of Almira! That was what I never forgave. And her, for preferring him to me and stepping out of her class. You go back to your way of life. I am sorry he did not marry my

112

poor girl for your sake, but you have no place here!"

"But Grandfather, I have no one else and neither have you! Could you not see into your heart to give me houseroom? I shall be no burden. I am to come into money."

"Money you say? You are not penniless? Ah, that could be different." His eyes gleamed and he looked from Louise to Mr Theobold. "And he, is he your intended?" Louise blushed.

"Of course not. I have just met Mr Theobold, who has been most kind."

The old man went to the door, and pulled it open sharply. The old woman nearly fell into the room.

"Nellie," he snarled. "How often do I have to tell you not to do that? Get some tea for us all, and have you anything to go with it? Some seed-cake or biscuits?"

"You know very well we haven't! You never wants cake. A bit of cheese now, and it a bit mouldy, or a slice of yesterday's ham."

"Stop yammering woman. Just bring

the tea then. We are not prepared for visitors." He turned again to Louise. "You can make do with tea. Now tell me about yourself."

"May we be seated then? It is bad manners to make us stand."

"Of course, of course. Anywhere you like. That young fellow is getting on my nerves prowling about, in any case."

"Sorry Sir." Mr Theobold blushed and sank into an uncomfortable high-backed chair.

"Now Miss, what did you say your name was?"

"I am known as Louise Belgower and always treated as Sir Timothy's daughter. My mother died before he could marry her."

"Yes, yes, I understand that. Useless young dog until the last."

"Please do not revile Papa. He was a very kind man."

"But couldn't make his mind up to marry her, and then couldn't decide what to do with you. He took the easy way out and just let you stay with him. Might I remind you he could have got the law in motion and adopted you legally? He was an indolent man!"

"Perhaps, but he was kind and I loved him. Then he married Mrs Agatha Treadgold five years ago, and now she wants me to marry her nephew. A man I hold in aversion."

"Agatha Treadgold? I seem to know the name. Was she not the mistress of the Marquis of Densburgh? He and I did business together." Louise coughed.

"Perhaps. I did hear some talk."

"So she married Sir Timothy Belgower! A dominating nasty shabrag of a woman. The Marquis almost came about after he got her off his neck. Poor fellow came a cropper over a younger bit of muslin. Shot himself finally. A pity. He owed me money!"

"After the marriage, nothing was the same. She made me feel inferior. She was always reminding me."

"Oh she was, was she? And now she wants you to marry her nephew. You must be worth quite a goodly sum of

115

money if she is keen for an inferior person marrying into her family."

"That is the whole crux! I was being held prisoner until I signed the contract, and the wedding was going to be in a month."

"It was begad?And so you took flight to me?"

"Yes, hoping my grandfather would do his duty by me. Can I hope?" She looked at him with tears in her eyes.

"Well, this establishment does not consider young females living in." He referred to Mr Jennings' letter again. "This letter says funds will be allowed you from a London banker at their discretion. In other words, if they approve of you living with a relative, all will be in order. You will not cost me money?"

"I assure you that was not my intent."

"And you will not disrupt my household? I live as it pleases me. I want no change, no upset."

"I will be a veritable mouse. You will not know I am there."

"Then you may stay. What about

116

your serving girl? Nellie says there is another young person. You will send her away?"

"Of course not. Where I live, Molly lives."

"We do not need another wench. Pay her off."

"I will not. I am fond of her. Besides," she said cunningly. "I am paying her, and she will help with your work. You will benefit."

"And she puts on no airs and graces?"

"No, she is a nice kind girl, and loyal."

"Very well, you may keep her, but remember, any trouble from either of you and you're out!"

Louise jumped up out of her chair and flung her arms around the old man, and kissed him on the cheek just above the scrubby whiskers.

"Oh thank you Grandfather. We will do nothing to offend you. Isn't he wonderful Mr Theobold? Don't you think him the nicest Grandfather anyone could have?"

"Ye-yes," muttered Mr Theobold, not sounding certain.

The old eyes looked Mr Theobold over carefully.

"And I shall not forget the part you played in all this, young Sir."

"I only tried to help. I did not set out to offend you."

"Offend? No Sir, you hear me wrong. I think you are an honourable gentleman to bring her here, knowing I knew you already."

"Sir, about the money, I mean to pay you. I come into my own money in ten months. I can repay the loan then, and the interest."

"Take no notice of the letter I sent you. Take your time dear boy. I think I have other plans for you. Do you want a further loan?"

Mr Theobold's jaw dropped. He could only stutter.

"Another loan, Mr Tyndal?"

"Yes. I would not like you to be embarrassed for money. I take it you will still be calling on my granddaughter?"

"Well yes, I suppose so. I really hadn't thought of it!" Then he grinned. "Of course Sir. What a fool I am. I should be honoured to call."

"Then another five thousand pounds will not come amiss?" He took a huge key from a drawer in his desk and moved to the corner of the room. "I do not as a rule open this safe while clients are here, but as you are nearly one of the family." The door which looked like any ordinary cupboard door opened and Mr Theobold caught a glimpse of an iron strong-box. Mr Tyndal picked up a large leather bag and weighed it consideringly in his hand. Then he put it on to a brass scale and added another handful of gold sovereigns, carefully noting the weight. "There you are young Sir, five thousand pounds in gold. Pass me that ledger, and I'll mark it up. If all goes as I want it to, I'll not charge you any interest. How's that?" He smiled and showed yellowed teeth amongst the many gaps.

"But-but — "

"Go along with you. Now Miss Louise

and I will have to get better acquainted. I'll instruct Nellie to give you the best room we have in the house. Run along young man, run along, and do look after that bag."

120

4

MR THEOBOLD was humming a little tune when he arrived back at Brook Street. His heart was lighter than for some long time past. The unsolicited loan of five thousand pounds had gone completely to his head. He even met a frowning Lord Falconer with no qualms whatsoever.

"So Marcus, you are not from home today? Are you not promised somewhere for dinner?"

"Yes I am. But I am awaiting the outcome of your foolhardiness. Did you find your lady-love a lodging?"

"Not so fast Marcus. She is no lady-love of mine. She happens to be a granddaughter of old Tyndal. Who would have thought a squinny old tough would have had so delectable a grandchild?"

"Not having the honour to do business with 'the squinny old tough' as you call him, I cannot say. I have heard of Mr Tyndal, who hasn't? And so Miss Belgower is his granddaughter! Strange, her not knowing his location. And that reminds me, there is an epistle here for you, delivered by hand, from the man in question. You must read it. The youth delivering it said it was important."

"Oh! Ah! Yes — er — yes. So I shall." Mr Theobold's fair features turned pink. "Of no consequence, I'm sure."

"Of course, you must read it. It must be important or he would never have had it delivered by hand! Are you in trouble?"

"No, no. Exceedingly well-placed at the moment, said Roland, thinking of the five thousand pounds concealed in the folds of his top cape. Very nonchalantly he opened the missive and read, and casually threw it into the log-fire. "Nothing to signify," and airily left the room.

Lord Falconer frowned. Roland was up to something. He could never remember the lad not being encumbered with some debt before. He noticed the missive had fallen short of the fire and slowly picked it up and smoothed it out. It bore out his worst fears. Josiah Tyndal was demanding payment on an unusually large amount.

He balled his fists, and slow anger swelled within him. And the young scoundrel lying in his teeth and not even turning his eyes away! He left the room and strode over to the wide curving staircase, to follow him and have it out. Then he thought he would be damned if he would run after him. One foot on the bottom step he stopped and bawled in stentorian tones.

"Roland, I want you down here, immediately. Roland, do you hear me?" A concerned butler hovered in the background, and he waved back a mob-capped figure who had come running at the disturbance. "If you don't come down here at once, I'll come up and horsewhip you!" Mr Theobold's valet appeared nervously at the top of the stairs.

"Beg pardon M'Lord, but Mr Roland

is in the midst of changing. He says he will be down, anon. He is having difficulty with his cravat."

"Very well, tell him I am waiting and to come as quick as he may." The man crept away.

It was a full half-hour before Mr Theobold strolled carelessly into the room, but Lord Falconer had taken the time to do some homework. Mr Theobold's bills for the last six months were laid out in front of him.

Mr Theobold quailed as he met his brother's grim look.

"Well?" he ground out. "What is the meaning of this?"

"Of what, dear brother are you talking about?" His chin was thrust out aggressively but the wavering eye belied the belligerence.

"Don't try coming to cuffs with me! You know what I am talking about. This bill, and this and this, and that pile of small bills over there. How can you tell me you are in exceeding fine pitch, when this is not the case?"

"Oh those, I can deal with them easily.

The others, they will all get paid. I have the means."

"Oh? I have not heard any great tales of you cleaning the board at White's! Have you come into money I know naught about?"

"Well, — er — no, that is — er no."

"Make your mind up. You sound as though you are not sure. And what about Tyndal's screed? He wrote rather strongly about your loan and the interest due. How about that?"

"You read my letter? You actually?"

"I did." Lord Falconer spoke calmly, but Mr Theobold was too indignant to notice warning signs of trouble to come. "Then I think you are beyond the pale. A real want of delicacy on your part and no gentleman. Marcus I am ashamed."

"Silence! You dare speak to me of the honour of a gentleman. I read your letter just to find out for myself just how deep in the bows you were. I find it very puzzling that you should keep assuring me of your so-called solvency. What do you say to that Sir?"

"I-I-."

"You cannot think a good enough excuse up quickly, can you Roland? How about the truth?"

"Well, I-er."

"Come on, man. As a man of honour and a member of this house, oblige me like acting like one. I want the truth!"

Mr Theobold shuffled his feet and looked at the ceiling for inspiration, and then caught Marcus' eye.

"Well, it's like this," and he went on to tell Marcus about the strange situation in Josiah Tyndal's house, and how at first he had not wanted to recognize Louise as his granddaughter. And how, when at last all had been revealed, and it was proved beyond doubt that she really was his granddaughter, he had changed his tune and offered Mr Theobold five thousand pounds in gold, and that if his plans went as he thought they would, it would be a loan without interest!"

"What?" Lord Falconer sat up straight. "You took extra money from him? And what were his plans eh?"

"He never revealed them." Mr Theobold looked decidedly uncomfortable. "I thought he was a little batty in the head."

"You are the nodcock! It smells like some kind of blackmail. Are you sure you did not offer for the wench?"

"Absolutely. Never mentioned a word. The last thing in my mind — My God! He did look a bit sly when I come to think of it. Said I was sure to be calling! I never thought."

"You never do," said my Lord bitterly. "I've never known such a skitter-witted knock-in-the-cradle as yourself! The next thing will be a summons for breach of promise or some such thing. Are you willing to marry her if the worst comes about?"

"M-Marry her?" Mr Theobold sounded frightened. "I don't want to get married! I only did her a good turn. I took her to her grandfather, that's all. Honest, Marcus, that was all there was to it. I dashed well nearly ran her over and she fell in the mud. She had nowhere to go and I brought her here to clean up. How was I to know that you would come home when you were not expected? Very remiss of you." He sounded like the injured party and his brother had to smile.

"And that is the truth? There was no tarradiddles between you? No sweet-nothings? No romps?"

"Nothing, I swear. And while we're on the subject I'm not — not — er, well, you know, up to snuff where the ladies are concerned. I'm no rake-shame. In fact, I've never," his colour came and went, and for a moment looked like the youth that he was, just out of the schoolroom.

Lord Falconer coughed, and waved a slim white hand.

"Time will alter that, but I have often wondered. About these debts, you will have to go on a repairing lease. That money will have to be returned. I, shall return it, with a piece of my mind."

"But you will show tact and decorum?

I do not want to be dunned for the rest of the money."

"We shall see about that. Perhaps some arrangement can be made and it can be paid out of the estate. I shall see."

"It is rather a lot."

"How much?"

"Well — "

"I said, how much?"

"Twenty thousand," said reluctantly.

"By Gad! You are worse than our father ever was! I thought he was bad enough. Cards I take it? If you have no experience of fast women."

"Yes. But never let it get out, there are no women!"

"Never. What do you think I am? I'm loyal, am I not?"

"Yes. You are good in your own way. But I wouldn't like Bunny and Monkey to find out."

"So boasting is one of your faults too, is it? Why get a reputation with women when it is not justified?"

"I suppose it makes one more interesting. Some of the young ladies will not look at one unless she thinks one is going to ravish her at any given moment."

"Faugh! They are not worth a second's thought. Grow up boy, and learn to do the things that will turn you into a man. Now, take boxing. Every man should be able to hold his own. And fencing, you are only fairly tolerable. I shall see about some lessons immediately."

"Yes Marcus." Roland seemed relieved to have got off lightly.

"What about Mr Tyndal then?"

"Leave Mr Tyndal and his granddaughter to me." Marcus spoke grimly. Roland did not know who to be sorry for. His brother would be a fair match for Mr Tyndal, but did his brother realize just what he was getting into? He grinned. He would dearly love to be the referee!

5

IT took Louise several days to settle in her new home. Her grandfather was wary and none too friendly. He resented the invasion of his privacy. He kept to the room he lived, ate and slept in and she saw little of him.

Nellie, the slatternly housekeeper, was openly hostile. She resented any criticism and change in her daily routine. The miserable kitchen-maid, Lottie, made shy advances to Molly, but was so woefully ignorant as to her proper duties it was appalling.

Louise, on a tour of the house, felt her heart sink. Apart from her grandfather's room and the kitchen, and Nellie's back room, it did not appear that any of the other rooms were ever used. Lottie lived out, and came by five o'clock every morning to light fires and take the housekeeper a dish of tea before she rose each morning.

Her own bedchamber was frowsty and cobwebbed. Faded bedcurtains and bedding smelt musty and above the window was a patch of green mould.

"Hm, gutters need attention," she muttered to Molly. "The first thing we must do is clean out this room. Tell Lottie to bring soap and water and a good stiff scrubbing brush."

By the end of the first day there was an improvement. Lottie stood, red, sore hands, beaming and bashful with the praise Louise heaped on her. She helped to carry back the feather bed, the quilts and linen that had been taken down to air by the kitchen fire. Nellie sniffed but offered no help. A truckle bed was put up in the same room for Molly.

"For the moment you will sleep here, until we can arrange for you a clean room. Perhaps you too would like to share with Molly?"

"Oh Miss, if only I could! There's no proper bed for me at home, and I have to start off at four o'clock to get here."

"Four o'clock? That is monstrous. Why could you not stay before?" Lottie twisted the corner of her sacking apron.

"She couldn't be bothered with me." Nodding her head kitchenwards. "It meant more food too, breakfast like."

"You mean you got no breakfast?"

"No Miss. Nothing till noon and then summat at six o'clock, usually leavings from Master's dinner, but sometimes I pinches a bite of cheese, or a slice of ham when she's sleeping. She sleeps a lot during the day. Gin, you know!"

"Then she actually does no work?"

"Oh no, Miss. I does it, leastways some of it. What I see' wants doing, but I'm not very good at it, and she gets fuddled."

"You have done your best Lottie. From now on I am going to change all that. There will be no more strong drink consumed during the day. I shall have a word with Nellie."

This she did, and an upset it was. Nellie was for packing her bag and leaving immediately. This Louise quite agreed with and was most cheerful about it. Nellie was shaken. After second thoughts she agreed to take orders from Louise.

"And your first orders Nellie, are to wash yourself all over and put on clean clothes, from the shift up!" Nellie bridled, but did as she was bid.

Louise surveyed the cellar-kitchen, noting the smoke-blackened lime-washed walls and the grease pitted on the stone-flagged floor and the dirty smears round the stone sink and on the dirty wooden table. A flour encrusted rolling-pin made her shudder. There were weevils in the crack of the handles!

She inspected the iron pans and found them fire-blackened on the outside and rimmed with grease on the inside. Lottie was a poor hand at washing up! She defended herself saying, "There's never plenty of hot water and no good soap and precious little washing soda. The only time we see yellow soap is when we wash the Master's clothes!"

"Well we are going to change all that. First of all Nellie, I want you to obtain a bucket of fresh lime. Fresh, mark you, steaming and not to be fobbed off with lime that has been laid around and lost its bite. The walls have to be washed all over until all is sweet and wholesome. They will dry white, but watch your hands or they will burn. Understand? And you, Lottie, I am making you responsible for seeing it is properly done. And after that, I want you to fill the sink with hot soapy water and wash everything in sight. Start with the glassware and cutlery, and work through all the china in the house and when your water grows cold, empty the sink and start again. I want everything gleaming and polished."

"Yes, Miss."

"And you, Molly, could you clean the brasses and those pans over there which I make no doubt are copper? I want shining brass candlesticks tonight for every one of us. I am going to check the other rooms. Look over the linen cupboard and count the stores in the pantry. Somehow, I think we are sadly lacking in foodstuffs."

135

Time passed swiftly. Louise overseeing, and Nellie grumbling, and the two young girls given to sudden bursts of laughter amidst the polishing and dusting.

Smells of better cooking wafted through the house, and grandfather Tyndal drawn forth, crept about watching and listening. First shaking his head in disapproval and wondering about the cost, and then as the fresh clean smell wafted to him, reluctantly nodding in admiration. There had been no requests for money, so he would rub his hands and go back to his office cum living-room.

Then one morning Louise realized the onslaught was over. The girls had moved into their own large room at the back of the house and a disused housekeeper's room cleaned and made habitable for them to use during their free time. Even Nellie approved, and was noticeably cleaner and friendlier.

The front parlour was much more attractive than its grimy exterior had promised, and the carpet had brightened dramatically with heavy brushing, and cleaning with soap and water — a process Lottie had never seen before.

Louise was quite pleased with the results. Now, the outside presented a nice neat appearance in keeping with the rest of Boss Lane. There was no need to be ashamed of the address.

She waited approbation from her grandfather. None came. He was still withdrawn and distant, very rarely interested or curious about her days. Then she took her courage in both hands.

"Grandfather, can Nellie and Lottie clean out your room?" She waited with bated breath and expected a storm. It came.

"Clean out my room! Are you mad? It is the way I like it. Do as you like with the rest of the house, but leave me alone."

"You would be far more comfortable."

"I am as comfortable as I am, thank you! You come here burdening yourself on me, trying to change my life, and telling my servants their duties! And

137

now you are wanting to interfere with my business!"

"Indeed I am not, grandfather. Nothing has passed my lips about your business, even if it is something I do not approve of."

"You do not approve hey? You have the effrontery to . . . to . . ." He spluttered into silence, his face an alarming shade of puce. "I call you an interfering female! You are interfering with my business. A moneylender always shows a shabby front to their clients, or they would never get their dues. It is no-wise prudent to show that one waxes fat on their apparent misfortune!"

"But you are, and you could live comfortably upstairs. Turn this room into a place of business only and live upstairs. I beg of you. You can still live privately if my presence distresses you."

"I did not say that! I have come round to a new way of thinking. I like having kin of my own. Give me time, child, to adjust. After her mother died, I made much of Almira. She was my all. She was cared for and educated far beyond the child of a draper. I made plans. She would marry into a higher class than ours. And it all came to naught and she broke my heart. Can you wonder I cannot change overnight?"

"Grandfather, I did not understand. I thought you never cared for her. Those letters."

"Written in bitterness. I regretted it many times but would never give in. Even a draper has pride! Many times I was tempted to find out whether I had a grandchild, and each time I shied away, frightened of further hurt."

"Oh Grandfather, what a waste. Papa was a kind man, he would have shared me with you. I know he would."

"We're all fools at some time or other. I am glad you found me, child. I can do a lot for you now." He squeezed her hand. "Has that nice young man called yet?"

"No Grandfather. Should he?"

"I thought he would have paid his respects. Do you like him?"

"He is very nice and polite. A trifle

young perhaps, but yes, I like him."

"Then you shall have him. He is of good family. I would be proud if you were wedded to him."

"Wedded to him? But grandfather, it never crossed my mind!"

"Then it should! You are twenty. A few more years and you will be an old maid. You do not want that?"

"No-o, but I do not want to be rushed."

"I want to see you settled. You are at a dangerous age. If you are like your mother — "

"My mother's only sin was to love too much and to be over-trusting. I am much more business-like than to let my heart rule my head! But I should want to marry for love."

"You are more like me. I like that. You are more decisive than your mother. You stand up to me. She never did. She just went away when I told her. If she had argued and stayed, things might have been different."

"I wish for your sake she had stayed.

140

And yet, I should never have known Papa, and I did love him."

"Well, there is no repining, but I can see that you have the very best and I'll see you marry well too. We must introduce you into society. I must know someone who can introduce you to the Patronesses of Almacks. If one of them vouches for you, you are in. Everyone will ply you with invitations." He walked up and down rasping his chin, a habit that still got on Louise's nerves. "Ah, I have it! The very person. Lady Norrington, a small waspish person, very given to playing Whist and Commerce and losing money. I help her out practically every month."

"But how?"

"By taking you about and introducing you. By being in the right place at the right time. Pass that ledger over. Yes, the one with the red leather cover. As I thought, in quite deep. She will do anything I ask."

"But will I like her? Will she be amiable?"

"She will. I will see to that. And as for liking, you need not worry about that. You don't have to like her."

"Oh, I would rather like her. It would be too embarrassing otherwise."

"Please yourself. Females are bad to understand." He shook his head and wandered to the door. "Oh, by the way, make up a bedchamber upstairs, and I shall start and eat my mutton in the dining-room. There, does that please you?" He smiled and shuffled away, shutting the door behind him.

Lady Norrington was small and dark with a poor skin, owing to much lead-based powder, and a way of screwing up her eyes which made Louise think she was short-sighted, but her dress sense was good and she introduced Louise to her milliner, her dressmaker and her hosier. They spent hours choosing new materials for gowns, and when Louise finally got a letter and a draft from Weber's bank, and also a stiff letter of disapproval, sent on from her stepmother, she really went ahead to produce a suitable wardrobe.

Molly was promoted to lady's maid, and found she had a natural gift for arranging hair. They took on another maid and a bootboy, which made Lottie's life easier.

One morning there was a ring at the front door bell. Louise wondered who the caller could be. Lottie answered the door and came back a little later to say that Lord Falconer had called to see Mr Tyndal. Her eyes were big and she looked impressed.

"Lawks! A real lord here! I've never talked to one before. He's big-like and wearing the most wonderful clothes. Dark green velvet with cuffs past his elbows and gold braid, and an embroidered waistcoat and all decked out with lace and such!"

"Where is he now Lottie?"

"In the front parlour Miss. Mr Tyndal has a client. He's got to wait."

"Then I must go to him and offer him a glass of Canary."

"Should I bring the best in Miss? That

in the decanter is the last of Nellie's buying."

"Yes. Wait a few minutes and then bring in the cut-glass decanter and the matching glasses on the silver tray, and mind you give it a quick polish before you do so."

"Very well, Miss."

Louise proceeded to the parlour and paused before she turned the handle. For some reason she was glad she was wearing one of her new gowns, a subtle apricot shade that complimented her chestnut hair. Fine ecru lace filled in the high neck and was repeated on the long, puffed sleeves. A knot of ribbon and lace was caught at the waist and she looked enchanting. She peeped at herself in the gilt-edged mirror just outside the door, well pleased with her appearance.

Lord Falconer was moodily looking out of the window when she opened the door and walked in. His hat and gold-topped cane reposed on a side table with a pair of exquisite white kid gloves. He whirled about quickly on her entrance

144

and frowned when he saw who it was.

"Lord Falconer, this is a surprise. My grandfather is engaged at the moment. Will you be seated?" She smiled up at him. He took her outstretched hand, and lightly touched the back with his mouth. She felt a slight tingling of the nerves. He straightened.

"Your servant Ma'am. Thank you." Sitting opposite one another with a table between they studied one another. He seemed larger than she remembered, and very distinguished. He was dressed to impress. Was he too riding for Dun Territory? She cast her eyes down, wishing she had remembered the new fan, and pleated her skirt instead.

She noted the sudden gleam in his eye when she caught him off guard and took a sudden breath.

"And have you got settled in Ma'am? Do you like London now you are staying permanently?"

"I have not been abroad much yet. I have been too busy with domestic matters. From what I have seen, London

145

is a dirty place, but I understand there are pretty parts. A walk beside the upper reaches of the Thames is to be recommended, and Vauxhall is to be seen to be appreciated."

"Well enough for the riff-raff, but young ladies like yourself should wear masques. And always have an escort Ma'am. It is a meeting-place for medical students and law students and the like, and anyone young enough to be high-spirited, and of course, their women. Perhaps you already know that?"

Louise blushed. It sounded very nearly as if he was reminding her of what he had thought she was! A slow anger made her appear sharp.

"No, I do not. I have not yet had occasion as I said to go abroad much. Some wine?" She rang the little brass bell, and Lottie must have been waiting outside, because the door burst open and Lottie staggered in laden down with two full decanters and several glasses on the largest tray in the house.

Only by a lifting of an eyebrow did

146

Lord Falconer betray any astonishment. Louise dare not look at him.

"You may go Lottie. Thank you. One decanter would have been enough."

"I brought the Canary Miss," and then her voice sank to a whisper. "I also brought the Master's best. He's a lord, you know!"

"Lottie! Yes, yes, thank you," Louise coughed, and then caught Lord Falconer's eye and suddenly she laughed.

"I'm sorry. Lottie is a good girl but unpolished. She needs much training and cannot cope with certain situations."

"Like entertaining lords, I presume?"

"Yes, she is a terrible snob. We shall have gone up ten-fold in her estimation. Will you have Canary or Grandfather's best French cognac?"

"Canary please. Thank you. Very nice." He placed the glass carefully in front of him. "Now Miss Belgower, I should very much like to ask you a question if I may?"

"Certainly, My Lord, if it is something I can answer, of course."

"What was your grandfather's object in offering my brother five thousand pounds in gold? I understand you were there when it was given."

"I do not know, sir. I was as amazed as Mr Theobold. I can only say that my grandfather acted most generously."

"But quite out of character. Has he mentioned it to you since?" Now Louise went white, and then scarlet. She remembered the conversation with her grandfather.

"I-I — ."

"I see you are confused. I cannot make up my mind about you. You appear a young lady of great innocence, and yet, I find you in compromising circumstances. Each time, there is an explanation. But now, I find this last, rather hard to swallow. You must be aware of your grandfather's intentions. Is he not trying to trap my brother into a marriage with you? Are you really the birdwitted innocent or as I said, a straw damsel, trying to catch a callow youth?"

Louise sprang to her feet, upsetting the clear amber liquid in her glass. It ran over the table and dripped on to her new gown.

"How dare you say such a thing? Am I never to be free of your insulting observations? If that is your true opinion of me I wish you good day, my lord." She turned on her heel and walked with stiff back to the door. "My grandfather will be with you presently." Her dignity deserted her when the door closed behind her. She flew up the stairs as if the Devil himself was after her.

She collapsed sobbing on the four-poster bed. She beat her pillows with clenched fists, and then sat up to find something to throw.

"I hate him, I hate him, I hate him!" and she caught up her silver-backed hairbrush and threw it across the room.

The door opened and a scared Molly peeked round the door.

"Oh Miss, you frightened me. Whatever in the world is the matter? Are you ill or something?"

"It's that — that — , oh never mind. I'll come about in a moment or two. I am vaporous exceedingly foolish."

"Shall I burn some feathers Miss, under your nose? They're good for the hysterics."

"I'm not hysterical Molly. Just leave me alone."

"Very well Miss. I only wanted to help." Molly flounced away, sulky and hurt.

"Molly!"

"Yes, Miss?"

"I'm sorry. I'm not on my high horse with you. I'm just — just — crotchety I fear."

"I think I understand, Miss. Ned used to upset me something cruel, he did."

"It isn't anything to do with anyone." Louise's voice was sharp. "It's me, only me."

"If that's what you say Miss. What about a nice pot of chocolate to sooth your sensibilities? And a nice piece of seed-cake to go with it?"

150

"Nothing thank you. I could not take anything."

"Then rest yourself, Miss. You are to go to Lady Marsham's tonight with Lady Norrington, remember?"

"Of course, and I shall wear the new organza gown sewn with pearls."

"Oh Miss, not the gauze that one can see through?"

"The very one. If I am to be considered fast, I may as well make my debut as a prime candidate for a bed-romp!"

"Miss, what are you talking about?" Molly was horrified.

"There are those who expect me to be a fair scandal-broth. We must not disappoint them, must we?"

"But you would not do anything wrong?" Molly gave a nervous giggle.

"No . . . o . . . I was brought up quite strictly, Molly. I know how to behave, but someone is going to get quite a shock. It could be quite amusing!" Yes, she reflected, for those with a sense of humour, quite amusing.

6

IT was to be Lady Norrington's first visit for dinner. They were to eat before going on to Lady Marsham's birthday Ball. Louise had dressed carefully and was pleased at the result, except, looking at herself in the long cheval mirror she did not recognize herself. But the effect she wanted was there, and that was all that mattered!

The white organza, with high waist and puffed demure sleeves was in direct contrast to the real effect of the gown. It showed every graceful line and contour. It hinted, it showed, and titillated but yet did not reveal. The deep plunging neckline brazenly showed two smooth pink cups with the bloom of young peaches. The bodice of the gown was sewn with pearls in scallops and here and there drops hung, scintillating in the candlelight. A demure single string of pearls encased her throat, choker-style, and her hair was upswept with side ringlets in the latest Grecian way. She was the essence of fresh innocence and wantonness.

Her grandfather peered closely at her, missing the gauzy outlines because of the lack of light. He liked what he saw.

"My dear, you are beautiful tonight. I am sure you will become the Toast of society. Perhaps even the Regent himself . . . "

"Grandfather, I shall never become another Mrs Fitzherbert. That poor lady has much to bear. His constant desertion for other women, and his maudlin reconciliations. Even we, in North Yorkshire heard of his monstrous way of life. And as for Princess Caroline," she sighed. "High-born ladies are not always to be envied, but even she, with all her dirt and slovenly ways has her compensations!"

"And you still hold with marrying for love, dear child?"

"Yes Grandfather. I am unfashionable,

I am sure, but I should still like to wed a man I could honour and love."

"A young man without many peccadillos behind him? Yes, Mr Theobold fits the bill. A pity he has not a title. I had in mind a certain duke for you, but now I see it would not serve. He is as old as I, and there have been two Duchesses already and a string of mistresses. No, Mr Theobold will have to do. I told Lord Falconer this, this very afternoon."

"Grandfather, what are you saying? Surely you do not talk of my nuptials to any other person! And Lord Falconer of all people!"

"He is the boy's guardian! I must talk to him if aught is to come of the affair. I must say he was most reluctant. He brought back the gold I gave the boy. Apologised for not coming sooner, but business on his estate kept him away from Town for a few days."

"Oh! That must account for Mr Theobold not calling. I did rather wonder and thought it rather remiss of him, even though I do not regard him as a close friend."

"You will, never fear," chuckled the old man.

"Why whatever do you mean?" Louise felt alarm. "I do not like all this talk of marrying him as if we were both some kind of merchandise to be disposed of to your satisfaction."

"You said you liked the boy. I have made my mind up you shall have him."

"But I don't want it to happen that way! I want to know my future husband and he to know me! I want to choose myself. Can you not understand?"

"I think you are spoilt. Your grandmother was chosen for me by my parents and we did very well. We came to love and respect each other. You will do the same."

"Mr Theobold is but a boy. I want more than that."

"You prefer the brother? The stern, proud Lord Falconer? A better match, but I cannot vouch for love on his side.

He holds you somewhat in aversion."

"No Grandfather. Definitely no! Please leave the subject of my marriage alone."

"A pity. Because I have Lord Falconer's reluctant consent to his brother paying you court. A consent, I might add, only given after a little pressure."

"What do you mean, pressure?"

"Oh, I'm not just a doddery old man with the gift for making money. I use my noddle. I have been busy these last few days. Old Josiah Tyndal is no fool! I've been busy buying up young Roland Theobold's debts! And now, when I say jump, he'll jump!"

"But that is blackmail, Grandfather! I do not want a puppet for a husband."

"Never fear, child. You will get a loving husband, or he will not have old Fox Tyndal's bottomless black stocking to fall back on."

"You mean you have actually arranged with Lord Falconer."

"Hinted, dear child. If I foreclose on young Theobold, it will mean all Lord Falconer's fortune too is gone."

"I do not understand. Mr Theobold is coming into his own money in ten months."

"So he keeps assuring me, but I have been making enquiries from my good friend Mr Smedley from the Royal London Bank where the Falconers bank. Mr Theobold has a happy knack of spending and gambling without adding up the cost. His debts far exceed his patrimony. A fact I pointed out to Lord Falconer."

"And what were his reactions?"

"Heh, heh, he tried his best to show no surprise or shock. One must admire his well-bred control, but I knew! He went white around the gills. Mr Theobold will be calling on you tomorrow!"

"It is monstrous. Grandfather, I will not have it. I feel humiliated. Surely I have looks and character to attract a man to me without recoursing to threats and melodramatic stratagems?"

"Of course, my child. I only make doubly certain. You will make a good alliance or my name is not Josiah Tyndal!"

There was a diversion. Molly gave a subdued knock on the door and entered.

"Lady Norrington is here, shall I show her in?"

"Of course," said old Josiah testily, but Louise was too quick. She met Lady Norrington at the door.

"My Lady, how well you look tonight! Come to the fire, you must be chilled."

"Indeed yes. A raw foggy night it is. Let me look at you." She raised her quizzing-glass and then let it fall. "My dear, are you wise? Do you not think your ensemble a little, er, risqué?"

"My dear lady, what do you mean? My granddaughter will be the new toast of London tomorrow." Old Josiah spoke proudly.

"Perhaps, but it depends on *how* she is toasted! That gown is definitely not Lady Marsham's style. Nor is it mine. Would you be good enough to change it?"

"Certainly not. Besides, our dinner awaits, and good food should never be treated churlishly. Come Grandfather, take Lady Norrington by the arm and I shall follow."

The dinner was good. It reflected Louise's good sense. She would make a good chatelaine reflected Lady Norrington. She knew how to handle servants, but her eyes strayed back to the gown. Who was she trying to attract? It might be quite an interesting evening.

The oyster soup was followed by salmon and several side dishes of cucumber and of almonds. Then there was a choice of pork roasted with apples served with spiced rowan jelly, a green goose and a side of beef with buttered parsnips, and a pottage of mixed vegetables well sprinkled with herbs. An egg custard, a cherry tart and three kinds of jelly and a rich cheesecake followed. There was both white and red French wine and some of old Josiah's best French cognac. And after it, a strong black coffee. Lady Norrington sat back, replete. If it had not been for her card losses and her being so much in debt she would rather have put her feet up and spent the evening gossiping around the huge log fire. She belched openly. Old Josiah beamed. It was a sign of contentment and a compliment.

"So you think my granddaughter is a beauty? She will cause a stir, I warrant. I think she does her grandfather much credit." Old Josiah was in an expansive mood.

"A veritable handsome wench, Sir, but the gown!" Her small eyes nearly disappeared in the wrinkles around her eyes. "Still, I'll say no more. I see the young lady has a mind of her own. The young must buy their own experience."

"Oh, come now M'Lady, I am assured that Louise is gowned in the first stare of fashion. You did assure me, Louise?"

"Of course, Grandfather. I think Lady Norrington is being a little overly cautious."

Lady Norrington glared at Louise but said no more about the gown. Soon, it was time to leave and Molly brought Louise her new evening pelisse, a long flowing brocade garment with a sack-back and held at the front with tiny pearl buttons.

It was lined with ermine and there was a hood that she could draw over her head if necessary. She was ready.

The old lady creaked and sighed, her whitened and painted face showing hard and old and world-weary, and by the side of the fresh young girl she felt tainted and decaying and the fact made her irritable, but she remained silent, her debts still on her mind.

Lady Norrington's coachman was waiting to hand them into the rather shabby old-fashioned coach. It smelled overwhelmingly of horses and was none too clean. Louise deduced that Lady Norrington's circumstances were certainly none too secure, and that when it came to a battle of wills, Louise would win, hands down! It made her feel better!

Lady Marsham's mansion was well lit. Each window and the opened door streamed light from myriads of candles in crystal chandaliers. Broughams, phaetons, hackneys and family coaches were lined up in front and each side of the great house in Stanton Square. Several powdered lackeys in blue and silver directed the flow of traffic and at once the coach was directed to the red carpet laid down the steps to the very edge of the road, so that no dainty feet would be muddied before entering the great double doors.

Louise was handed down by a young footman still unschooled as to appear unmoved at any sight. She was aware of his admiration by just a flicker of his eyes. It gave her confidence.

She followed the cerise-clad figure of Lady Norrington past the flunkeys and into the glittering atmosphere of one of London's most famous hostesses.

"My sweet Alice, how nice of you to bring your protegé! You are looking in spirits, and how well that cerise goes with your complexion! I must compliment you." The lady speaking these honeyed, but rather barbed words was Lady Marsham. Louise, rather frightened of the appraisal, curtsied correctly, smiled and muttered a greeting.

"So this is Miss Belgower. Hm, Alice, you played down her beauty! A deliciously fresh young lady, shy no doubt." Then as the fur-lined pelisse slid from Louise's shoulders and caught by a footman, her face changed. "Oh, I was mistaken! A high-flyer of the first stare. Come along my dear, I must introduce you to certain guests who will welcome you into our midst." She laughed and looked roguishly at Lady Norrington. "You naughty girl. I did not realize she was!" A playful poke with her fan said the rest. Lady Norrington compressed her lips.

"Indeed, Caroline, you are mistaken. This young lady . . . "

"What? In that neckline! I never make mistakes! Come along."

Louise glanced from her to the footman and then around at the company watching interestedly. Several gentlemen were regarding her through their quizzing-glasses. Two were smirking and preparing themselves for an introduction. She dropped her fan in confusion. Suddenly she felt as in a nightmare, and that she was suddenly transported naked from her bedroom to this colourful scene and that everybody in the world was looking and criticising her body. She was ashamed and wanted to run away and hide.

She followed the two ladies into the vast ballroom, her floating skirts tantalising and showing the lines of her legs. She wished desperately that she had never listened to that modish dressmaker who had told her that gauze was the latest fashion. A quick look round showed plenty of satins, muslins and silks but gauze was only being used as an overskirt. She bit her lip. She knew she had gone too far. No doubt in a certain quarter filmy gowns were the rage. She had wanted to cause a stir. She certainly had!

Introductions flowed over her. Names came and went, smiles and knowing nods from the gentlemen and frosty politeness from the ladies. A gentleman in long blue coat picked out in gold, and with the thinnest legs she had ever seen stood up with her in a quadrille. Then a small fat man in powdered periwig, plum coat and hot sweaty hands begged the honour of a turn at the cotillion, and before the dance was over, murmured something about supper later, and squeezing her hand in a suggestive way!

There followed several other eager men. Some young and women-weary, others as old as her grandfather with wrinkled white-powdered faces trying to appear young. They all had the same thing in common. All hoped for favours from this new fresh, (they hoped, nymphomaniac.)

At last she got away and found an ante-room where she was alone for a few moments. She fanned herself vigorously. There had been no sign of Alice Norrington who was supposed to be chaperoning her. And then she remembered the lady's passion for cards. Of course, there would be a card-school going somewhere! With a return of her composure, she rang for a servant, who directed her to a private apartment given over to the card enthusiasts.

Just as she was summoning up enough

courage to knock on the double-doors they burst open. Immediately there was the noise of laughter and talk. A resplendent figure in canary-yellow emerged, and staggering a little, turned to wave to his companions.

"Adieu! Until tomorrow. I shall meet you again at White's. Must pay my respects to-to-." His eye alighted on Louise. He looked her up and down.

"Well stap me! If it isn't Miss Belgower. The little lady I bowled over in the mud!"

"Mr Theobold!" Relief flooded through Louise. "Is Lady Norrington in there? May I go in?"

"Of course, of course! But you don't want to go in there and lose all your money! Sharks, the lot of them. Believe me I know. Just cleaned me out."

"Is Lady Norrington playing?"

"Yes, with all her old cronies. Sharks the lot of them." He hiccuped. "Pardon me, I have an affliction of the stomach."

"Nonsense! You're foxed!"

"That's right, and burnt to the socket!

166

What would you do? I haven't a feather to fly with," he said gloomily. "And it looks as if I am going to be leg-shackled before I've even had my fling."

Louise drew him aside and found a quiet sofa where she sat him down. He sighed and laid his head back and closed his eyes. For a long while there was quiet and then he spoke drowsily.

Leg-shackled. Me! and I swore an oath to my best friend Bunny Meadows that I would be a gay bachelor when I was forty! Hey-ho, what fortune does for a fellow."

"You mean your own stupid folly!"

Mr Theobold sat up with a jerk, and peered at Louise.

"I thought I knew that vinegary voice. The wench herself. Or am I dreaming?"

"Mr Theobold, I will have you know . . . "

"You will not have me anything! I haven't offered for you yet m'dear. Luck may change tomorrow."

"Mr Theobold will you listen? I do not want to marry you either."

"You don't?" Mr Theobold tried to focus his eyes on her. "I'm a good catch. No money, but good birth. You should want to marry me. Most remiss of you."

"But I thought you did not want to marry me?"

"That's right. I do not, emphatically not. You are a nice young female, none better, but I do not want leg-shackling. What a fate!"

"Then all is right between us. We both know how we stand."

"No. You should want to marry me! I take it as an insult that you do not."

"Mr Theobold, Sir, you are impossible. We must talk again when you are not out of wit!"

"I beg your pardon? I am in my right mind. Let us get this over. Will you marry me?"

There was a commotion farther along the corridor. The lights were dim, and Louise did not recognize the man in black velvet with silver points coming purposefully along the red carpet, but she recognized the voice!

"Aha! So I have found you both! Just in time I hear. Roland, might I ask you to desist? Have you accepted his offer, Ma'am?"

Louise's eyes flashed, and she stood up disdainfully swirling her skirts to turn away. He took her by the arm.

"Answer me Madam. It is vital to me."

"Unhand me, Sir. Why not ask your brother yourself, My Lord?" She cast him a contemptuous look and he stepped back.

"Because I want the answer from you. He is in no state to know what he is doing." He looked down in some anger at the somnolent figure who was snoring gently.

"Then all I shall say is that we talked of our mutual dislike of leg-shackling as he calls it. And he became indignant at my refusal of being his wife. Nothing more."

"And yet you compromise yourself by sitting alone with him in a quiet, sheltered place and I come along in time to hear him ask you to marry him. How do you answer that?"

"I do not need to answer it. The answer was no in any case. I think you as mifty as you are uncivil and as I have already observed, without conduct or delicacy!"

"Madam, you are very frank. May I also be frank?"

"Certainly if it makes you feel better."

"Then might I ask why you make your debut into society in such a blaze of notoriety? I hear of naught but the dashing Miss Belgower and the possibility of gaining her favours. In one night you have gained the publicity many matrons wish for but have not the nerve to emulate. Your gown for instance, would Sir Timothy have been proud of you now?"

"I-I-,"

"I see you have the grace to blush. I am no prude and do not set myself up to be a judge but no lady should deliberately give herself a reputation, before marriage. After," he shrugged, "that is a different situation, for which even I have taken advantage."

Louise pulled herself together. This detestable man with the worldly air needed a sharp set-down. She drew a deep breath ready to give him one. She let it out in a gasp when he said coolly.

"Miss Belgower, Louise, your grandfather is determined that you should marry a Falconer. Will you do me the honour of marrying me?"

7

LOUISE lay in the middle of the huge four-poster, cuddled well into the feather-bed and under the thick quilt. She lay thinking over the events of the evening before, half-exultant, half-apprehensive. She remembered the set-down she had given Lord Falconer and the astonishment and fury he had shown, and the feeling of triumph, but that had been short-lived.

She recalled his reactions when she had replied to his question, "Will you marry me?" with a contemptuous laugh and an equally contemptuous answer. "Marry you? I should lief marry a swine-herd!"

Quick as a flash he had grasped her to him, and looking down at her said grimly, "Probably so Madam, perhaps more to your station in life, but you will marry me!" His hands had burned her delicate shoulders, and she had felt their tingle straight to her heart. Their eyes had locked. His hard and determined, and hers? What had he seen in them, besides pride and temper?

Of one thing she was certain, she must avoid Lord Falconer as if he was the plague! She hated and detested him, and somehow the hating and the detesting was an ache. She could not understand herself. One moment, wanting to be with him, to bait and hurt, and another, to feel those remorseless hands cupping her shoulders and wondering what it would be like to be kissed. A pox on the man! she thought impatiently, and tried to put him out of her mind.

But there was another shock to come. She was enjoying her mid-morning chocolate and discussing clothes with Molly when old Nellie toiled upstairs panting and puffing, saying that Miss was wanted forthwith in the Master's office. What could grandfather want with her, that made the message so imperative?

She dressed in haste, but even so, with Molly doing up buttons and brushing and arranging her hair it was more than half an hour before she descended the staircase.

Listening at the office-door she could hear nothing but a low murmur of voices. So grandfather had someone with him! Suddenly her heart beat fast. Could it be? Taking a deep breath, she firmly opened the door and walked in. It was as she had suspected, Lord Falconer lounged on the settle near the fire.

He looked up and smiled grimly. Her answering smile was more of a quiver. Somehow she was trembling and could not control her legs.

"That is right my dear, sit down. We must have a serious talk." Her grandfather sounded pleased and he smiled broadly. "Lord Falconer has told me the news. You are to be congratulated. He offered for you last night. I must say I was surprised at his lack of convention and did not consult me first, but he has done the honourable thing and come post-haste this morning. Come, kiss me, my child."

"But Grandfather I do not — "

"I know you do not want an early marriage," interrupted Lord Falconer smoothly. "Your grandfather and I have discussed that already. We shall wait until after Lent and marry at Easter!" His smile held something of the fox with a rabbit. Her heart fluttered in her throat and she could not speak.

Her grandfather rubbed his hands, and then polished his steel-rimmed spectacles.

"Now we must have the contract drawn up. It can be done at any time to suit your convenience, Sir. You already know my terms." Then he turned to Louise. "It is fortunate that you are a willing party my dear. It saves young Mr Theobold from further embarrassment, and in Lord Falconer's view nothing will be revealed about your parentage, a subject I should not like to hear spoken of in the coffee-houses!"

"So that is how you persuaded my grandfather!" She whirled round, too angry to be frightened of this implacable man.

"My dear, he took no persuading. You must remember I am a better match than my brother. You should go on your knees and give thanks!"

"Never! Indeed I am at a loss to understand why you desire this marriage. As you say repeatedly, I am of low birth and do not even pretend to like you."

"If you do not know why I offered for you, perhaps in time you will come to realize. As for your birth, the world knows you for Sir Timothy Belgower's daughter."

"And an heiress in my own right. Is that the reason you had in mind, Sir?"

"It could be, I do not doubt, as your Grandfather and I have been discussing his dowry to you." Old Josiah had been watching first one and then the other.

"It is true, my child. All my wealth will come to you on my death, and on your marriage I will make over to Lord Falconer one hundred thousand pounds, and return all Mr Theobold's IOU's!"

"So the reason is money! I thought as much." Louise examined Lord Falconer's face for any sign, of what? Another reason rather than money? Stupid fool. What else would a man of the world like he was, want? It was money every time. Everyone knew that men in Lord Falconer's position married for money and then found their love and comfort elsewhere! Somehow, the idea hurt.

His look gave nothing away, and again their eyes locked, and she saw a sudden flicker in their depths. Did this man have a heart after all? The expression in his eyes made her blush. She said quietly. "Do what you will," and she left the room.

Somehow the rumour had already spread about her betrothal. No doubt Nellie had been listening at the door. But now, Nellie and Lottie and the bootboy were there to grin, and congratulate her, and Molly upstairs sighing with longing.

"It was so romantic, and he so handsome. How happy you must be, Miss!"

"Rubbish! I hardly know the man. He's a vain coxcomb. I'll make him wish he had not offered for me!"

"Miss!" Molly was horrified. "What talk is this? You want to marry, do you not? All ladies want to marry and have children."

"Faugh! A much over-rated pastime. Marriage does not attract me!"

"Oh Miss, to think I'd live to see the day! You will be well-cared for. He will be a kind husband, I'll be bound. He is not gross or fat, or coarse in his manners, and one can tell he takes a bath. What more do you want?"

I want to marry for love, Molly. I want to be swept off my feet and my groom to swear he cannot live without me. Is that asking too much Molly?" she said sadly.

"You have your priorities wrong, Miss. A lady marries a man of good birth so that her children also are of good birth. After that, she can always take a lover! Someone she really loves and money and position do not come into it." Louise rounded on her.

"Is that what you would do, in my place? You are as bad as my stepmother. She would not have minded my cuckholding her own nephew!"

"But it is the only sensible thing to do! How could a lady live with only her husband and no other diversions? It would be dull and life would have no savour."

"Is that how you would like your life to be?"

"I am in a different position Miss. I can do one of two things. I can marry a good honest man who can give me some comfort, such as a landlord or a well-heeled farmer or miller. I can work hard for him, and bear many children or I can become someone's mistress here in London. Enjoy a few years of luxury and if I am lucky, save something and become a housekeeper in my old age."

"And which do you prefer?" Molly giggled.

"I do not know. It depends who asks me!"

An announcement of the betrothal was

sent to the *Morning Post* and the *Weekly News,* and there was a round of parties and entertainments to endure. Lady Norrington decreed that more shopping was necessary, so numberless gowns and scarves, hats and fans and reticules were bought and several new pelisses and pairs of shoes. Lady Norrington so much admired a black fur cape that Louise made her a present of it.

A succession of presents arrived from Lord Falconer. A new enamelled snuff-box of the latest style. Louise's nose curled. She disliked snuff. A jewelled bottle to hold perfume, which she reluctantly liked, a Russian bearskin to use in the coach and several pieces of jewellery that were family heirlooms, and Louise thought privately, were rather vulgar, especially the heavy diamond necklace. And then he took her breath away by sending a posy of snowdrops and early indoor violets from the glasshouses of Falcon Park. With them came an oblique message that the flowers reminded him of her, whatever that meant.

And now began a time that was bitter-sweet. They met in the evening to attend routs and balls and once to meet friends at Vauxhall. That evening stood out in her memory. They all wore dominoes and dark cloaks, and spent the evening watching fireworks and eating in the private little booths dotted here and there in the great park. There were coconut shies and pie-stalls and stalls that sold oysters or muffins. The crowds were bibulous and shouted to each other. One crowd of students pushing and shoving, and baiting a number of apprentices. Scuffles broke out and the screams of women were muffled by kisses.

Louise was a little shocked and when she and Lord Falconer got separated from their friends became a little alarmed. But he swung her into a quiet path and their walk ended in a summer-house. Nervously she faced him. His face and eyes were in shadow, but the pale moon showed up her tiptilted face. His arms slipped around her and her eyes widened as his face came down to hers. His kiss was warm and tender, and then grew harder and more passionate. He kissed her neck, and his lips slid round to her throat and then her cleavage.

It was something she had never experienced before. Her heart felt like a fluttering dove. At first she fought him. Instinctively, she knew that this wild love was wrong. He was kissing her as if she was a wanton. Then the thought disappeared and she was left with only the thought that this was what she wanted. She kissed him back, and her body arched and moulded itself to his. She felt the hardness of him, and somehow knew that he wanted her as much as she wanted him. He trembled, and at that moment knew her hold over him.

Her arms crept around his neck of their own volition. She moaned incoherently, and her tongue sought his. Then he was fumbling and his hands seeking. It was as if someone had suddenly thrown cold water over them.

"Desist!" Her tone was suddenly sharp, and her teeth came together, nipping his mouth. He exclaimed and drew back. His face, flushed with passion, darkened.

"What is this? What have I done?" He held her to him, and searched her face for a reason.

"Take your hands off me. We are not married yet!"

"So that is it! I am surprised because you are no prude."

"You should not treat me so. I am no common tart to take advantage of!"

"You liked my loving! You did not say nay. You gave back kiss for kiss, caress for caress. You urged me on!"

"I did not know. I did not understand. Sir, take me home."

He took her face between his hands and turned her to face the moon. He looked down at her, and what he saw there made him catch his breath. She looked up fearlessly at him, two tears ready to cascade down her cheeks.

"Do you know you are very beautiful?" and then he kissed her gently and let her go. "Come I shall take you home."

But the memory of that night remained. He did not touch her again, but several times she caught his glance before he turned away, and her heart leapt.

Christmas came and went. It was spent in eating and drinking, entertaining and being entertained. Snow powdered the streets, and everywhere they went, great fires and spiced wine greeted them. The horses waiting to pull the large town-coach pawed the cobbles and their breath came forth as white steam.

Children and beggars stood by waiting for alms, and Louise felt guilty on having supped on fat goose, rounds of beef and legs of mutton. She gave freely, and to Josiah Tyndal's disgust, their house became a target for the poor.

Then one morning, Molly came all of a fluster. Louise, in her pale blue peignoir with the rose-pink ribbons was busy doing Nellie's accounts. Not being able to write, Nellie had peculiar ways of reminding herself of her purchases, such as a crust of bread and a lardy paper or a marrow-bone. She now stood with her basket of oddments and strove to remember anything else she had bought.

"Now think hard Nellie. There must have been something. There is a discrepancy of seven shillings and ninepence and one farthing. Come on think! What about wax candles and soap?" Nellie shook her head.

"No Miss, we bought candles and soap last week." She screwed her face up in an effort to think. She stopped and stared when Molly, puffing from running up the stairs leant against the door to recover.

"What ever is the matter Molly? You look as if you have seen a ghost!"

"Worse than that Miss. Oh dear! There was a loud banging on the door as well as the bell pulled. I answered as quick as I could like, but the banging started all over again. Very impatient he was."

"Who? Molly who?" Molly had an irritating habit of spinning out her news.

"Mr Holdsworth Miss," Molly's voice had deepened to a melodramatic whisper.

"He wanted to see Mr Tyndal right away, and was very much up in the boughs when I told him he would have to wait, as Master was busy."

"And where is he now, Molly?"

"Kicking his heels in the front parlour Miss, and not liking it by far!"

"Then I must go to him. Nellie, that is all for now. Try and think what else you bought, and we shall make up the account-book later."

"Ah, I remembered something Miss. I bought two mousetraps at the ironmongers and a bottle"

"Gin? I warned you Nellie!"

"It was for cooking with Miss," she said hastily.

"Cooking with? You don't cook with gin! Wine or cider, yes, but not gin."

"I do Miss. I get so hot cooking those there big roasts, and boiling those gert pots of ham I has gin to cool me off, like."

"Nellie, I've told you."

"Just a little one Miss, it makes cooking easier, it does!"

186

"Oh very well. Now go, and Molly, quickly, my dark green merino. I want to find out what that fat Georgie-Porgie wants with Grandfather."

"Nothing good anyhow Miss, I'll be bound!"

Mr George Holdsworth was sucking his cane and kicking moodily at the dismal fire when Louise entered the front parlour. He was quite a sight to behold. He looked fatter than when she had last seen him, and the new style of coat did nothing for his figure. A bright canary coat cut high with a deep collar that kept his head from turning easily gave him the look of a barnyard fowl. His buckskins were a shade too tight and his large thighs foreshortened his legs. His splendid waistcoat was striped in cream and gold and green and he sported a huge nosegay. A lace handkerchief in his hand matched the lace at his neck and wrists. He was aping the dandy, and put Louise in mind of someone about to offer. Offer! She took a step backwards.

His face lightened when he saw it was

she. Stepping forward as lightly as he was able he gave her a careful and stiff bow and kissed her hand. Her skin crawled at the touch of his lips, and at the same time she could hear the creak of his corset.

"Dear Miss Belgower, er — Louise, I can still call you Louise? I am in Town for some while and could not keep away from your side. I see you in bloom I trust?"

"Nothing has stopped you before from calling me Louise. I am well as you see. How is my stepmother?"

"Repining deeply. Never a day goes by that she does not mourn your loss. She is at this moment getting her town house in good repair. We entertain at the end of the month."

"I am not dead George. You make it sound as if I had gone beyond recall!"

"Alas, it seemed so to me, when you so cruelly ran away. Did you ever stop to think what the neighbours would say? You were very cruel to me, but I forgive you Louise, my dear, can we not be friends?"

188

"Friends? We were never so. Why all the loving attention? When you visited Belgower Towers all your interest was centred on the cock-fighting in the village. Has my stepmother sent you to me?" He flushed.

"She saw some ridiculous announcement in one of the London sheets. Some unknown friend posted it to her. She knows it cannot be true, but wants to nail the lie, and the mischievous person who sent it to her. It is ridiculous, I presume?"

"Of what piece of information are you alluding to?" Louise's voice was cool, and she preserved a discreet silence, only betraying herself by an impatient tapping of the foot.

"Oh my dear, it is nonsensical but there is an announcement of your betrothal to Lord Falconer, of all people."

"Yes, it is true." She faced him with proud eyes and steady look. "Why do you say of all people?"

"Because he is one of the proudest men in London. Birth means more to

189

him than love, or even country."

"What makes you say this thing?" She was shaken. He knew of her parentage. Why was he marrying her? She recalled his words when she had asked him the reason he was marrying her. "If you do not know the reason, perhaps in time." She frowned. Could it be? No, she was being foolish. It must be the money!

She watched George pace the floor with short pudgy strides. He turned impatiently.

"Everyone knows he was mad for Lady Jessica, and by some ill-fortune found out she was one of many daughters of Lady Fairweather, who were fathered by the groom, old Fairweather being impotent, after a fall from a horse."

"I do not believe you. If Lord Falconer drew back from an alliance there must be another reason!"

"That is the story, and when tackled, did not deny it."

"What happened to her?"

"She married soon after, and removed to some out of the way place in Scotland, no doubt mothering several sturdy brats by now!"

"And so you poke and pry and dig up this old tale. Why?"

"Why? You know why. Can't I sit down and make myself comfortable? And I would consider it more friendly if you offered me a drop of old Tyndal's best!"

"You can sit if you please, but you will get no wine here. I do not care to be friendly."

"Stap me, Louise," he protested. "We have got to be friendly! Aunt Agatha gave orders" He stopped.

"Do you think I am a birdwitted ninnyhammer? You think no more of me than before. Why do you let her bully you so?"

"I-I-", he gulped. Then he looked at her pleadingly. "I only want a quiet life. She is a very fine woman. Helped my mother when things went wrong, but very strong-minded. She had already sent an announcement to the *Yorkshire Star* and told her friends about our betrothal."

He looked away. "And has not told them otherwise."

"Not told them otherwise?" Louise jumped to her feet, startled and incredulous. "You are a nodcock! Why did you not refute the announcement yourself?"

"Because my pockets are to let. I've not a feather to fly with, and if I do not marry a rich heiress, I shall have to become a curate. Aunt Agatha threatens me."

"Oh, that odious woman! How poor Papa was inveigled into marrying her! It was always understood that she came from a wealthy family. She is nothing but a-" She stopped. Her look was a little kinder to George. Poor fellow! Caught by pride and a designing woman!

"Louise, could you bring yourself to marry me? It would release me from all my troubles. You could go your own way. Just think, the protection of my name, and free to live your own life. It is worth some thought."

"And in return, you and my stepmother would divide my fortune. Never! Besides, I am already betrothed."

"Not for long, my dear. Aunt Agatha will make it her business to tell him of your birth."

"He already knows. She will not surprise him!"

"Then she will make it known all over Town. It will make a rare scandal-broth. My Lord Falconer marrying a moneylender's daughter's bastard. It will even be whispered that he was bribed and coerced!"

"Why you fat pudding-heart, you nauseate me! Get out of here before I vomit! For one moment I felt some kindness for you. Now, I know you are as bad as she! Get out I say!" She looked wildly around and picked up a white porcelain figure and threw it at him. It missed him and crashed against the door scattering pieces around him, but it made him move swiftly, catching a boot-heel in the fringe of rug and thereby bumping his forehead on the door-lintel.

He was furious. Louise looked at him in surprise. It was the first time she had ever seen any emotion on his face, except frightened obsequiousness for his aunt. So the man was alive after all!

"You-you will be sorry for this! Wait until I tell Aunt."

"Go on, go crawling back to your aunt. Go on, weep on her shoulder. Act the spoilt little boy! Kick your heels and shout. She's more like your mother than your aunt!"

"How — how did you know?" Then he clapped a hand to his mouth. They stared at each other and then he opened the door so violently that it hit the wall behind it and brought a picture off the wall. The shattering of the glass and the earlier commotion brought Nellie and Lottie up from below-stairs and Molly from dusting the dining-parlour. They stood open-mouthed as he grabbed up his tricorne, and let himself out of the house.

Molly looked at the two other women.

"What are you two staring at? Get back to your work. There's plenty to do. Now Miss, what's all this?" She went into the front parlour and closed the door.

Louise looked at her and then started to laugh. She laughed so much that Molly was alarmed. Tears came, and Molly was for burning feathers.

"Lawks Miss, you do frighten me. Should I call the Master?"

"No Molly. I'll be fine. It's just, just — " She shook her head and then groaned in frustration. "To think I endured Lady Belgower's insults all those years! To think she could bait a young girl so, about — about — and she herself — Oh, it is most unfair!"

"There, there Miss. I don't know what you are on about, but I do know Lady Belgower was downright wicked in the way she treated you. All the servants talked about it, but no one dare speak up. Her London servants had long ears and we could have been turned off."

"I know Molly. Well, it is all in the past." She hugged the girl. "You were always a good friend, Molly. I don't know how I should have stood it sometimes, without you."

"You were good to me Miss. I'll not

forget you taking the blame when I broke that ornament on your what-not. She nearly bust a gut, I remember."

"Yes, my stepmother actually thought she owned all my personal effects. Even after she complained to Papa about my breaking the ornament and he told her I could break anything I pleased. It was mine and I could do anything I liked with it. Poor Papa, how often he was a buffer between us!"

"Aye, a good man, Sir Timothy. None better. A pity he married her. He might have been alive yet!"

"Molly!" She flushed and looked embarrassed, but defiant.

"It was what all the servants thought! Sir Timothy's own, that is. She nagged him to death, if nothing worse!"

"But it was his heart! The doctor said."

"Huh! That doctor! It wasn't old Doctor Penfold. I would have believed in him. It was that nasty shifty Doctor Trent Lady Belgower's doctor, and I wouldn't put it past him."

196

"That is a monstrous thing to say Molly!"

"Aye but the truth can be monstrous sometimes, Miss."

"Well, nothing can be proved now Molly. So we shall have to forget it."

But that was easier said than done. Louise brooded, and when Lord Falconer called, she was quiet and withdrawn.

"Something is wrong, Louise? Have I offended you in some way?" He was looking down at her, one arm extended along the mantle-shelf. His look was quizzical, but shrewd.

"Did you know my stepmother, Lady Belgower is now in London?"

"Yes, I think it has been mentioned."

"Do you know her?"

Lord Falconer frowned.

"Slightly. In days gone past she was a friend of the Marquis of Densburgh."

"Mistress you mean. Please do not wrap it up in clean linen."

"I have no intention to wrap anything up in clean linen where you are concerned. There will be only truth between us."

Their eyes locked like two rapiers. Hers were the first to drop and look away. She felt as if she was drowning in the depths of his. And their expression was hard to define. They appeared hot and yet withdrawn as if he was holding something back.

"My Lord."

"Call me Marcus. We are betrothed, remember?"

"Marcus, do you really want this betrothal? There is still time." He came to her and lifted her out of her chair and turned her to the light. His strong fingers grasped her chin in a cruel grip and he made her look at him.

"What is this? You find this betrothal so distasteful? I had imagined otherwise. That night at Vauxhall."

"Please, I want to forget that night. It was unseemly."

"And yet it happened. You cannot deny it. You cannot deny your own nature!"

"Are you suggesting because my mother . . . ."

"Of course not! You wilfully misunderstand. You were born of love. Why should you not have passions as other women?"

"Of lower-class women! Genteel women do not." He startled her by laughing loudly, a deep laugh of pure enjoyment. "You have a lot to learn. All women, ladies or otherwise, have their passions! Ask any rake in London!"

"And did you find Lady Jessica had her passions too?" a hard knot of jealousy swelled in her bosom, and she hung on his reply. He pushed her away.

"Lady Jessica? Who told you about her?" Louise was silent, and he shook her. His face had darkened and his voice furious. "Answer me, *who told you about her?*"

8

"**W**ELL? Did you impress Louise? You look downcast. I suppose you failed as usual." Lady Belgower's strident voice grated. George looked at her with distaste. Secretly, he detested her but feared to show it. Her bullying and the awful fact of her being indeed his mother, seemed to sap the manhood out of him. Breeding good cock-birds was much easier on the emotions. He reached out for his glass of Madeira, and absent-mindedly took one of Lady Belgower's ratafia biscuits. He wondered what her reaction would be if he took her by the neck and squeezed. He sighed. There would be no fear of that. He hardly dare think it, never mind doing it!

Lady Belgower looked at him with equal loathing. Her only son! It had been a mistake to dally with that youthful Mr

Felling. All romance and poetry. Well, she had been young herself. Everyone was entitled to one mistake! She had made sure there were no more, her heart being controlled by her head. She frowned. It had been another mistake to let her sister Lettie bring up the child. Her husband had been a vicar and she had carried on his ideals after his death, the result being a wishy-washy George who ate too much!

"George! How many times have I to tell you about nibbling? You are disgusting. Faugh! And you have the manners of a farmyard oaf. Now tell me about Louise. Is she in spirits?"

"Yes Mama."

"You forget yourself. I am your aunt. Never call me that name again. It could slip out in polite company."

"Yes Aunt."

"Well? Can you not speak?" She took a closer look "George is there something amiss? Nodcock! Tell me what happened at once!"

"Nothing, Aunt. I told her as you said

I should, that you mourned her loss. How you thought of her daily and how shocked you were at her disappearance."

"Yes, yes, and the rest, did you find out about the announcement?"

"It is true Aunt. She really is betrothed to Falconer!"

"The devil she is! Now I wonder how that happened. I do not remember Sir Timothy being acquainted with him. Well it will serve no purpose to refine on it now. Did you threaten her as I suggested?"

"Yes, and she laughed at me, and then grew angry," ht said moodily.

"She did eh? I shall settle her in a flea's leap! No chit will better me! I understand that lick-penny, Josiah Tyndal is a proud man in his own low-bred way. I shall call on him myself. You shall have the girl and Sir Timothy's money if I have to kidnap her myself!"

George thoroughly roused at this, looked worried.

"You are not thinking of kidnapping? Do you think she is worth it? After all, half of Sir Timothy's money considerable."

"You make me sick to my stomach. Kidnapping?" she laughed. "You absurd boy. You take me so literally." Then she stopped to consider, and then laughed again. "George, it might not be such a bad notion after all! Kidnapping! That could be the answer."

"Now look here, I'll not be a party to any kind of violence. Anything you do, I do not want to know about. If you can make her toe the line, I shall be happy, but — "

"God's teeth man! Mr Faintheart never won fair lady. But perhaps it would be better if you knew of naught that transpired. If I devise a plan, you must do what I say instantly. Do you hear?"

"Yes Aunt, but why kidnap her?"

"Because Lord Falconer will not marry a bride who is in the middle of that kind of scandal! Then you can step in nobly."

"You mean, I am not the man who will be doing the actual kidnapping?"

"Of course not, you have more hair than wit! Some unknown admirer full of unrequited passion will lose control and carry her off. You will step in to rescue her, and then we shall make it known, delicately of course, that she is defiled. Lord Falconer will not stand that. You will make her another offer, and if I know a despairing young girl's reaction, she will jump at the chance of marriage with you!"

"But Aunt, it is dangerous work."

"Come boy, do you or do you not want Sir Timothy's money?"

"Of course, what do you think?"

Lady Belgower looked around the front parlour with distaste as she waited to see Mr Tyndal. How any female could leave her beautiful home for this place was beyond her. Her lip curled, and she sniffed. Was there a slight smell of cabbage or drains under the beeswax? Or perhaps both? She settled herself squarely on the rather hard unyielding chair. Perhaps Louise would come down to speak with her. That Molly with the sly eyes would surely tell her she was here!

She considered Molly. The girl had shown surprise when she had answered the bell and saw who was standing there. But she herself, who prided herself on her reactions did not she was sure, show any sign of recognition of the little tweeny maid who had had the effrontery to leave her employ. If Louise had improved as much as Molly, perhaps she would have a harder task! But, she thought comfortingly, the kidnapping would settle young Louise!

She looked with some curiosity at Mr Tyndal when he entered the room slowly. He wore a velvet cap, but she could see his long silky hair was fine and white. A long thin face deeply grooved with bright fiercely blue eyes. They seemed to pierce one, like two rapier points. He would be a hard man to fool. He was no chaw-bacon, no slow-top, this man who lent money to his betters! He came forward and with courtly gesture brushed her outstretched hand with his lips.

"My Lady, this is an honour! Welcome to my humble house. May I offer you a glass of the best Madeira, or would you prefer a glass of lemonade?"

"Thank you, Madeira will do nicely." He rang the bell cord. Molly peeped in so quickly, Lady Belgower suspected she had been listening outside. Her lips tightened.

"Molly, the best Madeira please, and some macaroons for the lady." Molly's eyes widened. The best Madeira no less!

"Yes Sir," and with a quick bob left the room, but not before giving Lady Belgower a sidelong look.

Insolent girl, thought my lady, and tapped with her foot. She fidgeted, but could not find something to say and the old man was not forthcoming. It was after Molly had flounced in and laid the tray that she felt somewhat at ease. Sipping the wine, Lady Belgower decided it was finer than Sir Timothy's stock. She would dearly like to enquire who was his wine-merchant, but forebore. Probably smuggled, she thought nastily.

"Now my Lady, perhaps we can dispense with any further formalities and get down to the true reason for your visit."

This bluntness disconcerted Lady Belgower. She liked to call the tune and make everyone dance. This man indeed was no gentleman!

"Of course, Mr Tyndal. I am here on a delicate matter. Most unfortunate, I understand you have my step-daughter living with you." She coughed in a genteel fashion. "The naughty girl left my home in a freakish temper. I wonder that you did not advise me of the fact."

"Madam, of whom do you speak? You have no stepdaughter."

"Well, I-er-er, of course I have a step-daughter! I speak of Sir Timothy's daughter, Louise."

"The relationship is a matter of some delicacy. Pray let us both put our cards on the table. I know of you Lady Belgower. Pardon me, I should say all about you Lady Belgower. Do I make myself clear?"

"I am sure I do not know what you are talking about," she blustered.

"I think you do," he said quietly. "If you had come to me six weeks ago, I could not have cared what became of Louise. She was an embarrassment to a very proud hard man. Now I know her for what she truly is, a kind loving granddaughter, and no one, but *no one* shall hurt her! Now what do you want?"

"Do you know she is betrothed to my nephew? Do you want the scandal of her being branded as a jilt?"

"Madam, I am of an age when scandal no longer matters. But there will be no scandal." He held his head high, and his fierce blue eyes seemed to burn through her.

"What do you mean?" Her throat was suddenly dry.

"A whisper about my daughter, or my granddaughter and I shall have a word with Mr Fox, an estimable fellow to his friends but a master of the lampoon, and a scourge to his enemies! He takes great joy in hunting out old scandals, especially respectable persons' bastards!

"You wouldn't dare!" Lady Belgower's mind seethed. This clutch-fisted old goat was not bluffing. So Louise would also know that George was . . . she rallied a little. Lack of courage of a sort, was not one of her failings.

"You would risk Louise's marriage to Lord Falconer?"

"There is no risk. She is truly betrothed to him, and as for George, you must forget about any alliance with him."

"But we shall be the laughing stock of Yorkshire! Our neighbours expect a marriage to take place!"

"That is your worry. One should never count one's chickens."

"Oh, you are insufferable!" She stood up, prepared to go. "But one can never expect gentlemanly conduct from the lower classes! One cannot make silk purses out of sow's ears!" With that sally she sailed out of the room. Molly hastened before her to open the front door, and by her smile had heard everything. Lady Belgower could have smacked her face.

But there was still the kidnapping. She would go ahead with her plans. There was always some young buck with his pockets to let who would be willing to assist in that kind of adventure. There was the blond youth, George had met at Lady Sefton's. What was his name? Robert? no, Roland. Ah yes, Roland Theobold. Yes, a likely lad for that kind of adventure. As her coach trundled away, Lady Belgower licked her wounds and comforted herself. Yes, Roland Theobold was the man to help her!

9

"ANSWER me. Who told you about her?" Louise was appalled at the reaction Lord Falconer showed, at the sound of Lady Jessica's name. For one terrible moment she thought he would strike her, and she closed her eyes.

Nothing happened, but she was so close to him she could feel his heartbeats against her chest. She pulled away, and his hands went slack and she moved away. There was silence, and Louise stared at the carpet.

Then courage returning, at the continuing silence, she raised her eyes and spoke.

"George Holdsworth came to see me. My stepmother and he have seen the announcement about our betrothal."

"Have they, by Gad! And I suppose that was his way of causing trouble." The anger had died away, and he was very quiet.

"I think so, Marcus, who is Jessica?" She laid a timid hand on his arm. "Surely, if we are to wed, I should know?"

"She is none of your business, Louise," he grated. "She is part of my past, and finished with. A very lovely lady, who does not deserve that scandal should be dredged up again about her."

"You must love her very much," and a hard lump in Louise's throat threatened to choke her, and the pain in her heart increased.

"Love? I suppose so." He looked keenly at Louise. "If this matters so much to you Louise, I must clear up any mistaken conclusions. Come, sit beside me on this couch and I will explain."

Louise experienced a comfortable sensation of pleasure when they were seated together. The couch was narrow for two and she was conscious of his every movement. She wished she had her fan, for something to play with. Nervously she gave him a sideways look, but he was staring at the flickering fire, oblivious to her, or her nearness. She bit her lip and wished wholeheartedly that she had been the young Jessica. And that thought was a revelation. With sick fear, she knew she loved this man who was marrying her for her money! And whoever heard of wives loving husbands in these modern times! She was being missish and stupid!

But she thrilled when he took her hand.

"Louise, I am sorry for my anger, forgive me." He raised her hand to his lips and kissed it. Then he held it all the while he told her of Jessica.

"I said there should be truth between us. And I am sorry that for one moment I thought you were prying out of curiosity. Jessica is a childhood friend. We lived on neighbouring estates and shared the same dancing-master. She was like a sister to me. We played and quarrelled, rode together and climbed all the high trees in her garden and mine. We were promised to each other from infancy."

"You sound well-matched. I envy you

both." Louise's voice was drear.

"Ah, but wait! She was sixteen and I nineteen, when there was a great to-do between the two families. My father found out certain unforeseen circumstances about Jessica's Mama. I never knew whether they were true or not, but my father forbid any further connection between the two families."

"George told me the reason."

"Did he now? He has certainly been doing some spadework," said Lord Falconer grimly. Louise squeezed his hand.

"Do not say any more if it upsets you. I understand."

"No. You must know all. My father and I quarrelled, and he sent me away on the Grand Tour to make a clean break. While I was away, she was thrown in the hunting field and injured her back and legs. For a long while, I did not know, but in one of my mother's letters she referred to Jessica's accident. I came home despite protests from my strict Tutor. I found Jessica much changed.

From the laughing tomboy she had turned into a patient, uncomplaining cripple. Her mind was made up to being a spinster."

"And your father allowed your love affair to continue?"

"He did not know of my visits but something had died between us. There had been talk and she was ashamed. She fought my decision to go on as before. The boy and girl relationship was gone and we were as two strangers. Our conversation was made up of recollections of the past. Our laughter was of happenings long ago. There was no talk of our future together."

"Oh Marcus, how you must have suffered!" Louise wanted to weep for him.

"Not so much as you think. I found the thought of marriage to Jessica was becoming more and more a duty. I tried to hide it, but she knew. It was against all my honour as a gentleman to refuse her marriage, now that she was crippled. My father found out about my visits from one of the grooms, and there was hell to pay. He had a stroke, and remorseful, I brought in a new physician with new ideas. A man called James Crawford, a dour man but honest and blunt. He did for my father what old Dr Peabody could not do, frighten him into a better way of living. My father recovered, and I got the idea of Dr Crawford treating Jessica."

"And she recovered the use of her legs?" Louise's eyes shone. "Oh Marcus, did Jessica get better?"

"She improved, and with Doctor Crawford's new-fangled ways found she could walk again, slowly and painfully at first, but ever increasingly so. Then she called me to her one day. She had news for me. She was marrying Doctor Crawford and going back to Scotland with him. She was happier than she had ever been in her life. They were married quietly and within a month they were away. I was happy for her."

"Then everything turned out right for you."

"Yes, but my father talked, and though

he did not want me to marry her, he was displeased that she should want to marry someone else. He gave out the scurrilous story of my rejecting her through her birth. The scandalmongers had a field day. The Fairweathers never forgave him, and I never spoke to my father again. I came to London and set up my own establishment. Fortunately, I was wealthy in my own right from my maternal grandfather, and so suffered no hardship."

"Oh Marcus, what a lonely unhappy time you have been through!" He gazed deep into her eyes.

"Do not dramatize it Louise. I wasn't always alone! I have not been a saint my dear." Her eyes dropped at the look in his, and his arm came about her shoulders. "Louise, when we are married . . . " His arm tightened round her.

But there was an interruption. She would never know what he was going to say. Molly knocked and came into the room.

"Sorry Miss, to disturb you, but Lady Belgower is without, and wishes to see you."

"Oh!" Louise looked bewildered, first at Molly then Marcus. He moved away from her. The spell was broken.

"I think, my dear, you had better see her." He consulted his timepiece, "I have an appointment at White's in just under an hour, so I will see you tomorrow." He smiled and added under his breath so Molly should not hear. "Remind me to tell you how beautiful you are." The look in his eyes drew a delicate flush to her cheeks. He kissed her hand, and was it her imagination that he lingered over it?

"Very well, Molly, show her in. My Lord is just leaving." When Molly had hastened away, Marcus quickly kissed the tip of her nose.

"Until tomorrow then. We have much to talk about."

She was smiling when Lady Belgower entered the parlour. Lady Belgower's eyes narrowed ever so slightly. She had

218

encountered Lord Falconer in the hall and accorded him the stiffest of bows. Now, she took in the slight flush and the lovelight in the chit's eyes. The silly wench was in love with the man!

Louise thought her entrance somewhat theatrical. Mrs Siddons in every gesture! Not for the first time, she wondered whether her stepmother had walked the boards of some theatre. There was much about her she did not know.

"Ah my dear, how wonderful you look! Naughty child for not coming and paying your respects! See, I have had to come myself. I have worried about you constantly since you so ungallantly left the Towers. And at last I could stand it no longer, I had to come, only to set my mind at rest. Dear Louise, say that we are not enemies. What is gone, is gone. Now we must be friends, for I am a lonely old woman."

Louise listened with amazement and then nearly laughed at the 'lonely old woman' piece! If anyone but herself had described her as a lonely old woman she would have been affronted. Agatha Belgower still regarded herself as an attractive woman, mature certainly, but attractive, as she had once misguidedly confided to her best friend, Lady Weldon. It had been the talk of the town for several days, and there had been a constant stream of male visitors at her door for a while. That fact had not made her furious, but the wagers, the bucks and rakes had made were humiliating.

But Louise composed her features. It was no use opening hostilities again if her offer of friendship was genuine. Somehow she did not think so. It sounded too rehearsed. Again the theatrical touch!

"Please be seated Lady Belgower. Would you care for tea or a glass of wine perhaps and some cakes?" At a nod from Lady Belgower, Louise motioned to the goggling Molly.

"The best Madeira, Molly and some of Nellie's curd tarts, if you please. Go on, hurry now." She gave Molly a quelling look and Molly fled.

Lady Belgower gave a leisurely look

around, and then looked Louise up and down.

"I see a vast improvement in you, Louise. You appear to have more countenance. It becomes you. You have the makings of a good wife. I congratulate you!"

"Lady Belgower, I suspect you are throwing the hatchet at me. You need not butter your words to me, and I am not a simple pea-goose who can be flattered."

"My dear, as if I should."

"Well, Lady Belgower, why did you come to see me?"

"My dear girl, why so formal? I am here for your own good. I am not flattering you. I speak the truth when I say you will make a good wife." She stopped as Molly came into the room and waited until they were alone again. She watched Louise and her graceful actions as she poured wine and proferred a dish of sugar cakes and tarts. The wench certainly had an air of breeding.

Then she settled back and sipped her wine. Once again her thoughts turned to that common little man and his good wine. Ah well, one couldn't have everything! She looked across at Louise and they were like two swordsmen waiting for an opening. Louise waited, serene in the knowledge that her patience would be rewarded.

Soon enough, Lady Belgower spoke her mind. Sipping delicately she said,

"Your grandfather is a connoisseur of wine. I must congratulate him on his cellar."

"I think you already have done so, Madam. Would you like me to send for him now? He would be delighted to meet you again, I am sure." Her hand hovered near the bell-cord.

"No, do not fetch him from his business. I know he is a busy man," smirking nastily. "My visit is with you entirely."

"Oh yes?" Louise was determined not to be drawn. The bitch could come at it in her own way!

"Now that the subject of your betrothal is a public fact, I should like it excessively if I could help you in preparing for the wedding. Would you like that? The Belgowers must stand firm against the world. Do you agree?"

"Ye-es, I suppose so." Louise was not at all sure however. Her brain raced. Where was the catch?

Lady Belgower smiled, showing her large teeth. Horse-faced, was Louise's silent conclusion. And her very attempts at conciliation made her uneasy.

"Then I should deem it an honour to provide your bride's clothes."

"But there is no need. I myself as you know, am independent." Lady Belgower laid a hand on Louise's arm.

"But I insist. A gift. A token that all is well between us. Remember, I have no daughter of my own to spoil and cosset!"

Cosset! Louise could only stare. This was coming a bit too fine! She was more suspicious than ever.

"Very well, if you insist. Thank you.

I take it kindly of you."

Lady Belgower beamed.

"There now, I knew we should come about. And to seal our friendship I am giving a party on the Monday of next week. I hear the large pond on the Heath is frozen. I intend to hold a skating party. It is now fashionable to hold such parties. I think it will be entertaining. Will you come?"

"Thank you, yes. It is a long time since I skated, but I warrant I shall not have lost my skill. I see there are skates to be bought in the city. It will be most diverting."

"Very well then. We meet at three o'clock. My servants will build a fire and there will be spitted meats and heated pasties and hot toddies, and plenty of fur wraps for those who do not skate but take a little airing around the pond, and it is the fashionable thing to have several spare coaches for persons desirous of sitting out of the wind. I will arrange it so."

"I see you will become the most

popular hostess in Town."

"You think so?" She bridled at the implied compliment. "I am to outdo Lady Jersey for original parties. Now that I am living permanently in London, I mean to be the most outstanding hostess!"

"And if you put your mind to it Madam, indeed you will!"

Lady Belgower again took this to be a compliment. "Dear child, I really think we are beginning to understand each other. Now I must be off. I must call on Lady Sefton and leave my card."

Louise escorted her to the door and into the hall. Mollie hovering, opened the door. Lady Belgower looked at her and her nostrils quivered.

"Really Louise, you should employ a butler. It is not fitting you should only have this — this . . . " Words failed her and she shrugged. "I shall see to it, you have a butler. I will contact the agency."

"There is no need, Madam," Louise's voice was tight and cold. "We are comfortable as we are. We do not

225

entertain much. There would be nothing for a butler to do."

"But for your own consequence! I do not know what your grandfather is thinking of."

"Might I remind you that my grandfather thinks nothing of consequence! His tastes are simple and so are mine."

"Oh well, I suppose your plebeian instincts must come out. However, you are still Sir Timothy's child and somewhere about you must be the gentility of your breeding."

"Thank you Madam for your kind words. Then you think there is hope for me?"

Lady Belgower was considering the possibility in a serious way when she saw the light of battle in Louise's eye, and coughed.

"Ah, um — well, I shall leave you now. It will make me very happy to see you on Monday afternoon." She descended the steps to her carriage.

"And Lord Falconer too, I trust?" called Louise, but Lady Belgower did not hear, or if she did, did not look behind.

Thoughtfully, Louise watched the carriage drive away. She had been half-inclined to believe her stepmother's assertion to become friends. Against her judgement, she had been half-persuaded to believe her. After all, it would be an embarrassment if the Polite World knew there was antagonism between them. Lady Belgower would not like that.

But the little episode concerning Molly showed that the good lady had not changed. Sometime during that interview, Lady Belgower had become angry and had not showed it. She had taken it out on poor Molly, and then could not resist the barbed shaft of her birth. She shrugged and moved into the hall allowing Molly to close the door. It would do no harm to go to Lady Belgower's skating party, after all! Perhaps she might even find out what all this was about!

It was a very thoughtful Louise who went to find her grandfather and tell him of her invitation.

10

LORD FALCONER left the house in Boss Street, slightly disturbed. He wondered what mischief was afoot. Lady Belgower had a reputation for being a formidable woman. Why the pleasant morning call? He was uneasy, especially when he had just got a little closer to Louise. A pity Lady Belgower had chosen that moment to call. He and Louise were just on the brink of a better understanding.

White's was as busy as usual. Several gentlemen waved a greeting, and all the talk was of high wagers, the latest mill with Battling Bert from Battersea, Tom Mellincourt's attempted suicide, (found hanging by his current mistress and cut down) and the latest crop of bankrupts. Also mentioned in passing, the Regent's latest extravagance in the Pavilion at Brighton.

There was talk, too, of the United States declaring war on Britain because of the blockade, and several gentlemen were worried about the effect on their business interests. Normally, mention of business and trade was taboo, but times were changing and many a good man could go under. Someone remarked it was a pity Mr Pitt had died. "A wily bird and a scoundrel, but he would have known how to handle those American upstarts. A political argument broke out, and Lord Falconer went to wait for his friend in the reading-room. He looked at his timepiece, Richard was late.

There was someone else waiting in the reading-room. The hunched figure started up in some surprise when he saw him.

"Marcus! Just the man I want." Young Roland Theobold's face lit up. "I've been looking all over town for you."

"Well young sprig, you've found me. What do you want?"

"The strangest thing's happened. I wanted some advice."

229

"Must be strange, you don't often want advice."

"Well this time I do! Remember that mill that was advertised last week in Battersea?"

"Yes, I meant to go and see it. The chaps were on about it. Battling Bert and Rough-house Baker, I recollect."

"A good match. Mind, I think Baker should have dashed well won it, but Battling Bert has a great bunch of fives, and Baker's right eyebrow was cut."

"Is that all you have to tell me? I'm supposed to be meeting Richard here."

"Richard Trenholme? I've got a message for you. He said he couldn't wait. He's got a wager on. Who can tool down to Windsor in a curricle in one day."

"He's mad to try in this weather. I hope his Tiger has taken a spade to dig him out."

"Didn't say anything about taking his Tiger, but he was bosky before he started!"

"Damn the fellow. I hope I haven't to go after him."

"And that reminds me of what I have to tell you."

"Damme, I hope you have not been getting into one of your usual tarradiddles!"

"Now don't set up your bristles. Nothing's happened yet. But as I was saying when you interrupted . . ."

"Me interrupt! I like that. You were drivelling on about the Battersea mill."

"Yes, and if only Baker had given him a leveller with his left . . ."

"Roland, stop wasting my time. What are you about to tell me?"

"Oh, didn't I tell you? It's George Holdsworth."

"What's he got to do with Battling Bert?"

"Nothing." Roland looked puzzled. "I was only telling you where I was when I ran into him. We met earlier at some rout I forget which. Queer bird. Made out we were bosom-bows. I swear I only ran into him a couple of times at the most. Now, he makes out we are pages one and two!"

"Why?" Lord Falconer's question was

clipped and brusque. Roland looked uneasily at him.

"I assure you it was all his idea. I only agreed, to quieten him."

"Roland, stop being a pudding-head and tell me properly from the beginning. What did the shab-rag want?"

"He gave me some tale about being madly in love with some fair charmer and that she was ready and willing to elope. I am to drive off with her, because her family must not know he is involved. He offered me a thousand pounds to do it." He flushed at the look on his brother's face. "You must admit Marcus, a thousand pounds is a lot of blunt."

"Aye, but the reason for offering it must be shady. If the family do not want the match, you would do well to keep out of it."

"I have given my word."

"Dunderhead, are your wits addled! If the family found out it was you who eloped with her and the Bow Street Runners were called in, they would have a case against you. Who is the girl?"

"The girl's name was never mentioned. He would point her out to me."

"And where would that be, might I ask?"

"On Hampstead Heath. Monday night to be precise."

"The fat George must be in a hurry. How are you to go about it?"

"I am to wait in a coach, away from the fires that are to be lit. Someone is to take her skating on the pond there, and lose her. Then at a given time, some great lumbering fellow is going to frighten her towards my coach. After that, it will be a matter of me overpowering her and driving off to an arranged spot where George will take over."

"It does not sound as if the wench will go willingly."

"George says it is all play-acting to satisfy anyone watching."

"I don't like it Roland. You would do well to retract."

"I gave my word."

"Then it is on your own head. I for one

do not believe that ramshackle fellow, and I think you a regular chaw-bacon if you do, but it is your affair!" He shrugged and turned away.

Later, speaking with Louise he was not so certain that it was not his affair. She was pleased to see him, and as they were both bespoken for Lady Sefton's rout, travelled together in his coach. He was looking very splendid in black velvet and tight buckskins, with diamonds twinkling in his lace cravat and on his fingers. His waistcoat was of silver and black brocade, the very latest from Mr Weston.

Louise admired his appearance and told him so. She hoped it would encourage that feeling of friendship they had found earlier.

"The black and silver becomes you vastly Marcus. I shall have to watch you and all the other young unattached females. They will be making eyes at you I fancy."

"Could it be that you could possibly be a little jealous?"

"My Lord." He shook his head and pursed his lips. So hastily she amended it. "Marcus, it would be unseemly for me to object. We are not yet wed. Otherwise," She fluttered her ivory fan and looked roguish. He pulled her to him and kissed her ear.

"Have I ever told you, you look beautiful in dark cherry red? And in truth, any colour you choose to wear." She looked mischievously at him, her face framed in fox-fur.

"You once asked me to remind you to tell me how beautiful I am. Do you not think my nose and mouth too big?"

"Certainly not, they are you. And your beauty is my kind of beauty. We shall make a good pair. Strong and bold, and handsome. Not pretty, but handsome!"

"I have heard it said that handsome covers a lot of ground. Many women are described as handsome when it would be imprudent to call them pretty."

"Now, now, Louise. You are fishing for compliments. It is enough that I consider my future wife beautiful. Red becomes you."

"Thank you kind Sir. I will make a note of it."

"Red is warm and loving. Just the colour for a cold February day or night."

"And that reminds me Marcus, have you had an invitation from my stepmother to a skating party for Monday? These parties are all the rage at the moment. Everyone is either giving one or attending one. Do you skate?"

"A skating party?" He frowned and appeared abstracted. "Yes, I skate. Who else will be there?" Louise laughed.

"Oh, the world and his wife I should think. It will be quite a big affair. My stepmother has at last held out a hand in friendship. That is why she called yesterday. Marcus, what is the matter?"

"Nothing my dear." He looked at her strangely. "No, I have not had the honour of an invitation."

"Oh Marcus, how remiss of her! It must be an oversight." But the memory returned of her calling after her stepmother.

"Has Lord Falconer an invitation?" And her stepmother not looking back or answering. "You can always come with me. You will not be noticed in the crowd. Besides, it will be dark, and all the flambeaux in the world will not light up all the shadows!"

"No my dear, a Falconer does not go without an invitation!"

"Then I shall not see you on Monday night?" A note of disappointment was in her voice.

"No. Will you miss me?"

"Of course. I like your protection."

"Is that all? Just my protection?"

Louise blushed.

"I-I — You should not ask such personal questions." She twirled her fan to hide her confusion.

"Louise," he hesitated, and then drew a deep breath, "just how well do you know George Holdsworth?"

"How well? What do you mean?" She sounded as bewildered as she looked. She had been expecting some kind of a declaration. To mention George was

237

like cold water in her face.

"I mean just that." His voice sounded grim. She was not to know that her confusion could be mistaken for guilt. A monstrous idea, born of jealousy was consuming him. He must know!

"I-I-have met him on several occasions at Belgower Towers. He is my stepmother's . . ." She hesitated. It could do no good to repeat what she knew.

"I am not concerned with who he is, I am only concerned in what he is to you!" Louise stared in the gloom of the coach. His face was a blur. She badly wanted to read his expression. She moved away, and he felt the movement and was sick at heart. Anger welled up in him. So there was a plot after all! And yet, the young female, so eager to elope with George Holdsworth had not been named! He could be mistaken. It could be some other misguided wench!

Louise was silent. Shock made speaking impossible. A darting searing thought went through her. He had once before

238

accused her of being a straw damsel! Was he always going to distrust her? If so, it would be as well to find out now, and break the contract. Better a jilt, than a distrusted wife! Gathering the shreds of pride around her, she turned on him.

"What he is to me! What do you think he is? Answer me. Do you think you are a cuckold before you are even a husband?"

"By God, if I thought I was . . ." His hands gripped her arms and he turned her to him so she was half-laid over his knee. "I warn you Louise, no tricks. I'll not have a wife who plays the field. What I have I hold."

"I'm not yours to have — yet."

"Ah, so you do mean to . . ."

The coach stopped and a flunkey opened the door to hand Louise down. She stepped out with dignity, and with stiff back climbed the carpeted stairway to Lady Sefton's well lit residence. Lord Falconer, frowning, followed behind.

The rest of the evening was a disaster as far as Louise was concerned. Louise took refuge amongst the dowagers and Lord Falconer disappeared to play whist. A fact noticed by several malicious young ladies and their mamas. Lady Norrington came fussing over to her. She was unhappy at the fact that Louise had come in the company of Lord Falconer and not herself.

For once Louise was pleased to see her, and promised faithfully to go home with her. At midnight sandwiches and coffee were served in the huge dining-room. Louise and Lady Norrington partaking together. Now, Lady Norrington was beginning to wonder. She eyed Louise narrowly.

"Have you and my Lord quarrelled, or is he in the process of changing his mind? Some gentlemen can never be relied on. I think he is a born bachelor. Mark my words he is going to cry off!" There was a little note of satisfaction in the voice.

"As if I should care either way! Lord Falconer is nobody special. There are plenty of fish in the . . ." Her voice tailed away. She had turned to place her plate on a convenient sidetable, and there he was, looking for her and carrying two glasses of champagne. She faltered and looked down. She felt his glance on the top of her head. Then she saw him turn away and stride purposefully from the dining-room and through the double doors into the ball-room. He did not look back. She ran a few steps after him.

"Marcus!" He must have heard, but he went on.

"Odd's bodkins!" breathed Lady Norrington, "I would never have believed he had such temper! My dear, you may be better off without him."

Louise turned away with a sob.

"I want to go home. Please take me home Lady Norrington. There is nothing for me here!"

11

LOUISE had spent two restless nights and Monday morning found her heavy-eyed and listless. There was no sign of Marcus and the day before had dragged. She wondered drearily if all was over between them, and was the contract broken? The little sleep she had succeeded in having had been punctuated with nightmares. A vengeful crowd parting to give way to her, crying "Straw Damsel! Straw Damsel! and jeering and laughing and spitting. She had awakened in a sweat and found herself bolt upright in bed, trembling and shaken.

She spent her morning as usual, lazily and discussing with Nellie the affairs of the household. Grandfather and she had come to an admirable arrangement. They both cared for their own privacy, so they met only for meals, breakfast excluded.

Grandfather breakfasted early and then took a walk before the stench of the day, as he put it.

Lady Norrington called, with the sole reason of finding out the details of the quarrel. She was all agog.

"My dear, you look wan. I take it there has been no Lord Falconer?" Louise numbly shook her head. "Then take it my dear, the betrothal is at an end. I doubted the stability of the affair from the start. Make no mistake, he has had second thoughts. Your birth you know!" She gave a nod and a knowing wink. Louise drew herself up, anger giving place to despair. Lady Norrington was an odious, interfering old harridan!

"Lady Norrington, do you mind leaving this house? And please, never return. I can dispense with your services."

"Well really! The impertinence of young people these days. I only said — "

"I heard you Madam, and take great exception. I think you most uncivil and rag-mannered. Any coldness in my relationship with Lord Falconer is my affair I think, not yours."

"Don't you get into a pelter with me my girl! I was warned what to expect, in chaperoning a girl of lower birth. I belittle myself as to take the job, but through the persuasions of your grandfather."

"Persuasions? My grandfather ordered you to! Have you forgotten your debt to him?"

"That does it! No genteel young lady would mention such a thing. I shall leave at once."

"Good. Good morning Lady Norrington. I shall pay your reckoning just as soon as I have been to the bank. I will send it by messenger. Molly, show Lady Norrington out!"

The lady shook her shoulders, settled her pelisse firmly and throwing Louise one last venemous look stalked out, head high.

There, that's the end of any chaperone, thought Louise suddenly a little lighter-hearted. Without being aware of it, Lady Norrington had depressed her. It had taken a great effort to be cordial with her. Now there was no need to keep up any pretence. There was no need for a chaperone either. Her spirits dropped. Now she would become just another old maid, who cuddled a King Charles spaniel for company, and got more and more vinegary as the years sped by. The picture made her sniff. It was enough to make any female with sensibilities cry.

However, as the time approached to meet her stepmother, perversely, Louise determined to enjoy herself. She dressed with care and chose a heavy wool skirt in scarlet with matching jacket in a military style. There was black frogging down the front, and a frothy white cravat peeped out from below her chin. A dashing black hat in the shape of a gentleman's tricorne completed the ensemble. It was embellished with a long scarlet feather which curled down to her shoulder. She was pleased with the effect and twirled several times in front of the long cheval mirror.

"Oh Miss, you look wonderful. What

about a patch under your eye?"

"No. It may come off in the wind and cold. Better leave it. I shall want my fur gauntlets, and the fur cape. It could be cold when we eat."

"Aye, and you'll take your foot-warmer and the fur rug. We don't want you catching a cold on your lungs, now do we?"

"Dear Molly, you look after me well. By the way, have you any shopping to do today?" Molly blushed.

"I was going to ask you if you wanted anything at the apothecary's shop."

"Nothing thank you. I have all the unguents and herbals I need. You have shopped there a lot lately." She noticed Molly's confusion and a little smile played about her mouth. "He's nice. Why don't you ask him to tea? Nellie could prepare something in the housekeeper's room."

"Oh Miss, could I? Do you think she would mind? Or do you think it would be too forward of me to ask him?"

"Maybe a little forward. How long has

this been going on? Probably he needs a push."

"Five or six weeks. We only speak in the shop. He is Mr Trimble's nephew, and learning the business."

"Then take the rest of the day off, and go and buy me some cough cure. I shall surely have cold when I return!" She laughed, "It is not like you Molly to be so coy."

"I think he is very nice. I would not like to offend him in any way."

"In other words, you love him?" Molly nodded.

"Oh yes," she whispered, "very, very much."

"And you wouldn't mind being his wife, and bearing his children, and forgetting any silly thoughts about being someone's mistress?"

"Oh Miss," giggled Molly. "That seems a long time ago. Now, I think it would be Heaven to knit Tom's socks and patch his shirts!"

"Then you must be in love. Go to it Molly, but I'll miss you."

"But he might not think the same way as I do Miss!"

"Silly girl! Of course you know. Do you not watch his eyes?"

"Yes. They light up when he sees me, and he smiles in welcome."

"Then he is a man in love. What are you waiting for?"

There was a half-hour to spare before going to Hampstead Heath. She would go and find grandfather, and talk to him for a while. She seemed to neglect the old man lately, but he did not appear to mind. His world was so different from hers.

She found him dozing in what he termed his office. A blazing fire always made the room uncomfortably hot, but that was the way he liked it. His blood ran cold. He was happiest amongst his papers and files. The flat-topped table he used as a desk was crammed with documents, some even piled on the floor. And there was a ledger, big and fat and open as if he had been adding something to someone's account.

He awakened with a start. He looked as guilty as a little boy caught in the jam cupboard. She smiled down at him.

"Do not stir. You look most comfortable. May I sit and talk a while?" He sat up however, and rubbed his eyes.

"Have I been asleep? Must have been the fire. Nellie will keep it high. I often tell her."

"And quite right too. You need forty winks once in a while." He smiled ruefully.

"I can't hoodwink you. You know my ways now. It is the advantage of old age. I enjoy those forty winks." They smiled at each other, comfortable in their relationship. He looked her over, noticing her outdoor garments.

"You look very fetching my dear. Going somewhere special?"

"Lady Belgower's skating party on Hampstead Heath."

"Ah yes, are you wise?"

"Wise? You mean the weather? It is still frosty, and there is no sign of snow, or a thaw. I think it will be diverting. Did you skate as a young man, Grandfather?"

"There was no time for such follies. I was too busy making a poor living. My mother had eleven children, and five died. There was no time for frivolity. Every penny counted." His tone was grim. Louise looked at him in surprise.

"Why Grandfather, do you disapprove of my social life?"

"Not as such. But I disapprove of wild flirtations and any threat of personal dishonour."

"Grandfather, what are you saying?"

"I have had a visitor this morning and I heard a strange tale. I see you are dressed for a long journey. Is this little talk of ours, a goodbye?"

"Now you are talking in riddles. Are you quite well? Can I get you some hartshorn or a little brandy?"

"Do not try and divert me, child. I know all is not right between you and his Lordship, but you have not come up with any kind of a solution. An alliance with Lady Belgower again will not serve. I warn you!"

"But it was only an act of kindness on her part. I take it as a kind of truce. Is that so bad?"

"And what of George Holdsworth? Are you not playing with fire?"

"George Holdsworth? He has nothing to do with me! Just because my stepmother holds her hand out in friendship, does not mean to signify."

Nellie poked her head round the door and nodded her head unceremoniously back over.

"A gentleman out here to see you Sir. He says it's urgent. Keeps threatening to commit suicide, he do. I told him not on my clean floor. Miss would be shocked, I says."

"Very well, Nellie show him in. Now my dear, be careful and think well about your actions. Do nothing you will regret." He kissed her on the forehead, and she left the room puzzled. It was as if he thought she was leaving forever.

The late afternoon sun shone on the frosty ground making a continuous fairy-like glitter. The coach moved at a fair pace, the road being firm for travelling. Now and again it lurched into a particularly deep rut, and then the cries of the coachman and the light whip-crack on the slipping sliding horses encouraged them to pull even harder.

The road was quiet. No one was abroad on foot. The cold was intense and the rime on the fields and road made it a strange new silent world. Louise peeped out, and saw icicles hanging from the roof of a barn and passing a pump saw the drip had frozen to a good two feet in length. A cobweb in the hedgerow glistened jewel-like in the rays of the setting sun. Soon it would be colder.

Then in the distance could be seen an orange glow in the sky and there was the smell of wood smoke. Soon, the deserted Heath was deserted no longer. She stared at the rows of coaches, traps, barouches and phaetons. All the world seemed to be skating on Blackberry Pond! The coachman pulled in near the ornate coach of the Belgowers. It was easily recognizable in its blue and gold paint.

Stable lads were already running to take the horses, to be rubbed down, fed and covered with blankets. Sheaves of straw had been built up to protect the horses from the wind. There was a smell of horse manure and sweat. Now and again there was the clank of harness and a groom's soothing, "Whoa lass."

Now, a horse nickered as their horses were led away. The coach, bereft of the high-stepping pair was now just so much lumber among a lot more lumber. The coaches spread in a mighty circle around the pond, and judging by certain sounds coming from some, made useful boudoirs.

Louise picked her way to the two great bonfires burning near by. She could see Lady Belgower sitting, swathed in fur in a sleigh shaped like a huge canoe. She waved to Louise.

"Hello there, come for a ride across the pond. There is room for one more." Louise stepped up gingerly. Already there were two young ladies giggling in the back, and two gentlemen sitting in front. She squeezed in beside Lady Belgower.

"Isn't this capital? The sleigh is Lord Belfont's, and under right conditions he races with it." The sleigh, drawn by four black horses moved away. Round and round they went, circling the pond and the skaters dodged out of the way as they passed by, calling and waving at their friends.

"Is the ice safe?" shouted Louise above the hubbub.

"Perfectly my dear. You may have no qualms. They say it is frozen solid in the middle. Have you brought your skates?"

"Yes. I shall take a turn later. They are only old wooden ones, but will serve. How exciting it is. Are all these people your friends?" Lady Belgower shook her head.

"Not so. There are at least three parties here. And I suspect quite a lot of gatecrashers. We shall have to be careful." She waved to a girl dressed all in white, wearing an ermine tippet and a huge muff to match. "Trust the young Duchess of Sheldon to be a good skater! A regular show-off. Look, she is flirting with Lord Whylie."

It was as she said. Louise could see that there was something going on. A vision in bright green kept pace for a while with the sleigh and then dropped behind, to swerve to a standstill by a wondrous figure in yellow and orange. "Judith Hart, the best kept woman in Town, with Mr Molesborough," hissed Lady Belgower. "One of the richest men, with the least brain. If she manages to land him, she's made for life!"

Louise's mouth was one large O. So many people she did not know, and all a trifle risqué! The sleigh pulled in beside the huge bonfire. Already the servants were hacking off large joints from the roasting ox. A smell of burning beef mingled with the odour of spiced mulled ale. Louise realized that nearly everybody, especially the men, were a trifle foxed. And, surprisingly, was Lady Belgower. This was something she had not seen in her father's time. Sir Timothy had frowned on anything that could develop into an orgy. Or had she been too young to understand?

It was when she was struggling into her skates that George Holdsworth came over to her. His great coat was dark, and he was dressed more for riding rather than skating. But he offered to hold her hand while she tried out her legs.

"I think I can manage George, thank you." She lurched as she spoke and grabbed him. "On second thoughts I might find it prudent to hold your hand."

"Then we shall take a turn around the pond. Look over there someone is executing the most amazing turns." For a moment, they watched and then joined the skaters who were moving smoothly around the perimeter.

Louise enjoyed the sensation of flying through the air. The cold wind whistled, and she was pleased she had the forethought to pin her hat on securely. She slipped her hand out of George's and glided away confidently on her own.

Looking around she saw she had lost George, but was not worried. There were too many people about to get into difficulties. She tried a few experimental steps. Yes, it was all coming back to her now. She tried a twirl and sat down hard on the ground. A figure in black skated up and stopped with a rasp of iron on ice. He bent to pull her to her feet. The flickering light of the bonfire lit up his face.

"You!" Her heart gave a great leap of gladness. It was Lord Falconer and he looked grim. Her heart sank again. It did not look as if he had come specially to see her!

"Are you hurt?" The tone was abrupt.

"No, only my pride. I thought I was a good skater."

"I saw you holding hands with young Holdsworth."

"Yes. He was very kind and held me until I could control my feet."

"Where is he now? Skulking in the darkness I suppose?"

"I'm afraid I lost him. It does not matter." she said lightly.

"Oh? Did you not come with him?"

"No. I am Lady Belgower's guest."

"Then I shall escort you to her. It is dangerous to skate away from the light and on one's own."

"I think you are being overly anxious. What harm can come to me?" He shrugged.

"I suppose it is a matter of what you call harm. None, I hope."

"You talk in riddles, like my grandfather. Marcus?" But he turned away, waving and replying to a passing acquaintance. The unspoken plea was not heard.

As soon as they moved into the circle of light and amongst Lady Belgower's party, Lord Falconer glided away. Louise was conscious of disappointment. He might have stayed and offered to make up their quarrel! She sighed. He had changed after all. The feeling he had for her had not been very deep.

A tall thin gentleman in rusty brown claimed her for a dance. Two fiddlers had struck up a merry tune, and several couples were already waltzing together. He was elderly and his legs long and reminded Louise of a big spider or daddy-longlegs but he could dance gracefully and she enjoyed it very much.

Two other gentlemen claimed her, and then she stopped, panting and exhausted to eat. Lady Belgower's servants plied them all with champagne or coffee or brandy, whichever was preferred. Louise found a plate of beef and pickles thrust into her hand. Lady Belgower fussed her and teased her for flirting with all her friends.

"Indeed not Ma'am. I was asked to dance. I did so to be polite." The man in the rusty brown came over to her.

"Will you honour me again Miss Belgower?" He did not wait for her reply but swung her out on the ice once again.

This time, the ice had fewer skaters. They whirled around faster and faster. And then, all of a sudden they stopped and the stranger laughed and lifted her onto the side of the pond. They were well away from the lights and it was lonely. No other skaters happened to be there. There were thickets at that side of the pond and some scrubby trees. Suddenly she was alarmed. Nobody had noticed them skating away in the darkness.

She felt foolish. The man was friendly enough. There would be some perfectly good explanation! She looked up at him.

"You are a friend of Lady Belgower's?"

"No. Never seen her before in my life." He laughed down at her. "I'm here doing a job if you must know."

"What do you mean, a job?" Now she was really frightened.

"I'm here to see you safely delivered into a certain coach at eight o'clock precisely. It is now about five minutes of the hour. It should be here soon." His grip on her arm tightened.

"Are you mad? Do you mean to say you are kidnapping me?"

"Holding you, lady, for someone else to kidnap. I deliver you into the coach and my job's done. I can go back to the others, and no worry."

"Who's paying you to do this thing?" He shrugged.

"You must know your admirers better than I. Now which one would you like it to be?"

"Insolent dog! Let go my arm or I shall scream."

"Do so, and this might go off." Something hard rammed itself into her side. She looked down with horror at the horse-pistol held in a firm hand.

"Why you — you . . . " Words failed her. The cold cut into her bones. Skating, she had been warm. Now, she was rapidly cooling down and her teeth chattered.

The man appeared to be listening. Then of a sudden he pushed her up the bank. They stumbled over frozen tuffets of dead coarse grass and dead roots of trees and finally came out on to a rough cart track. There was the sound of wheels on the frozen earth, and out of the blackness came a coach. It was a hired hackney, and smelled of musty hay and sweaty horses. It stopped beside them and the stranger peered up at the coachman.

"You up there, have you the gold I was promised?" The coachman, his head swathed in top hat and scarves against the cold did not answer, but he tossed down a bag that clinked. He weighed it in his hand and nodded his head. "Right. Where do you want her, inside? Hey! anyone in there to hold her?" The coach door opened silently and a figure beckoned. "There you are Sir, all right and tight. One little lady, paid for and delivered." He sounded cheerfully casual, as if he did this sort of thing every day of his life.

Louise struggled as he lifted her up into the coach. She caught his thumb in her mouth, and bit on it hard. She tasted salt and knew she had drawn blood. He screamed and then his other hand came up, and she fell forward, senseless. But as she swam away into blackness, her last thought was of the pleasure it had given her to bite. It was a great satisfaction.

Her head was aching dreadfully when

she finally came round. The steady jog of the horses reminded her of what had happened. She was not tied up in any way, and was pleasurably comfortable in someone's arms. Startled, she looked up and at once drowned in a pair of brown eyes. They glinted strangely in the light of the moon.

She groaned and gasped and then struggled to a sitting position.

"You, my Lord! What happened? You are the last person I expected to see. Where is that horrible man?"

"He got away, and with the gold. Are you disappointed? Did you think it would be your lover?"

"What do you mean, my lover?"

"You were about to elope with George Holdsworth. A mistake, Louise. I keep what is mine!"

"Elope with George? You must be deranged. I would never — "

"Then explain your first captor. Why did he bring you to the coach?"

"Because you paid him. I heard the clink of gold . . . your gold!"

"Not my gold. Holdsworth gold."

"But I don't understand. *You* are kidnapping me. Please tell your coachman to return to the rout. It is madness taking me away. My reputation will be in shreds."

"I think that is the main reason for this charade." He knocked on the ceiling of the coach and the trapdoor opened.

"Yes? What do you want?" The voice sounded familiar.

"Stop at once. There is a lot of explaining to do. Put on the brake and tie the reins to the post and get in here."

"Who is that?" whispered Louise.

"My brother, Roland. Now we shall get at the truth."

They sat silent while Roland made the horses safe, and then he climbed in beside them, blowing on his frozen hands.

"Mighty cold out there. Hello Louise. So it was you we were to pick up. The sly devil! So it was George and you all the time. Why not accept him at the very first? Did you want him to run after you, or were you just playing hard to get?"

"Roland Theobold, I know nothing of this. And I do not like your levity. The situation I am in is no joke. If this escapade leaks out I am undone. Who will want a wife who is the cause for scandal?"

"That's quite enough. You will still marry me. If I did not know otherwise, I should say you are having an attack of the vapours."

"Never! I want to know just what is happening. Mr Theobold, or may I call you Roland? Please tell me."

"George Holdsworth came to me and asked me if I wanted to earn a thousand pounds. Naturally, I said yes. I'm always game when it's a matter of making a little of the ready. I was to bring the coach and another man to the sound side of the pond and wait near the old blasted oak tree. It was to be nigh on eight o'clock, and the young woman he was going to elope with would appear with an escort at precisely that time. He mentioned no names. Just that she was willing."

"But it's not true! I have long held him in strong dislike. Nothing in this world would make me elope with him!"

"Is this true Louise?"

"Oh my dear, do you doubt me? Do you not see?"

"Forgive me my dearest. I am a jealous brute. These last days have been torture to me."

"Then you *do* love me! I did not know."

"Silly little fool! Of course I love you! Would I insist on marrying you otherwise? Why do you think I have been so frightened of losing you?"

"Dearest."

"My darling."

"Will you two lovebirds stop the cackle? Aw, you make me want to puke. We've still got to catch George, and Lady Belgower in the act. What about it?"

"Oh Marcus, can we not just go home?

I want no fuss dear."

"You want them both off your back, do you not?"

"It would be better so. What can we do?"

"Carry on with the plan. Roland, where are you to take Louise?"

"Back to town, but to put up at the Rose and Crown in Islington. But what of the man whose place you took? Will he blow the gaff to George?"

"Not he! I pelted him a leveller, and ducked him in the horse trough farther back along the road. I gave him a half sovereign. He'll either be frozen by now, or drinking ale in his favourite tavern. There is no danger there. So it is back to the Rose and Crown, Roland."

"It is cold out there, how about you taking the reins?"

"Not this trip sonny. You are the paid coachman, remember? I shall look after Louise. Now get moving!"

"Oh very well. Remember you owe me a favour." He climbed out of the coach and then turned to Louise. "Did

I tell you, you are my favourite sister-in-law to be?" He squeezed her hand. "We'll nobble both George and his so called Aunt!"

The coach rumbled on its way and Louise, now about exhausted with the unaccustomed exercise and excitement started to tremble and her head ached. Marcus wrapped her tenderly in a checked wool rug that smelt as if it had last been on one of the horse's backs, and then kept a loving arm about her.

"Rest a while. You are all a tremble. Once we get to the inn and trap George, then I shall drive you home."

She must have dozed a little because it did not seem so very long before the coach pulled up in the inn yard. A sleepy ostler appeared from the stable, and the inn door was flung open by the fat landlord.

"Welcome, welcome. You need rooms for the night? And food? I can give you cold cutlets, a succulent ham basted with honey and brown sugar and the best of a joint of beef, served with parsnips and other roots and a goodly mince pie of my good wife's making. There be a posset for the lady, and good wine and brandy for yourself."

"And my good friend the coachman!" Marcus grinned at Roland.

"That puts me in my place. Tell him."

"Tell him nothing. Do you want him to talk to George? Surprise is our best bet."

"Ah, I see the strategy, and also the fact I shall be skulking in the stable for the next few hours!"

"You may. On the other hand you could make a few friends in the Tap."

"The Tap! How revolting! But I suppose I must if you say so."

"I do say so. Perhaps the success of the plan depends on you."

The innkeeper's wife was very helpful. There was a bedchamber with a fire already on. It was bespoken, she explained, which made Louise wonder if it had been originally for her! She lent Louise a comb and brought water to wash with,

269

and saw she drank her posset. It was reviving and by the time she was ready to descend the stairs she felt a new person.

The meal was delicious, and afterwards she sat in the inglenook, watching the play of the firelight on Marcus' face. For the first time she experienced what it could be like married to Marcus. Theirs would be no marriage of convenience, she was sure.

"Marcus," she held out a shy hand and he took it gently.

"Yes dearest?"

"When we marry, will you want to stay on in London? I find the social life tedious. I prefer the country. Sometimes I long for Yorkshire."

"Dearest, I am a country man myself. In fact, I have a confession to make. I followed you to London from York. I changed my journey."

"My dear, I did not know you had an estate so far North. Why did you not tell me?"

"I was not sure of you. I thought

perhaps you preferred London."

"There are so many things we do not know about each other. Where is this estate you speak of?"

"To the west of Harrogate. A few miles into pleasant parkland. You will like it excessively. It was mother's home and left to me. Ravensleigh House. A great house set amongst a great people. Yorkshire men and women are the salt of the earth."

"Then I shall find friends there?"

"Surely. I am all eagerness to introduce you."

There was a commotion in the inn yard. At once, Lord Falconer reached the door and peered out. A coach and steaming horses were drawn up. He saw Roland talking with a muffled figure and guessed that George Holdsworth had come for Louise.

He whirled and picked up his broad-brimmed hat and cane. His many caped coat he slung over one shoulder.

"Quickly, set yourself in woeful attitude. Do not look so happy my love. You have a visitor. Be not afraid. I shall be without."

"But Marcus!"

"Courage my love. Here he comes!"

There was the sound of a door crashing back on its hinges, and a voice shouted.

"Ho there Landlord! You have a room bespoken for me?" and the sound of running feet. Louise recognized George's rather high pitched voice.

"Yes, Sir! A fire is lit and all is ready."

"And the wench?" The answering voice was lower. It whispered.

"Damn the man's impertinence! Ate with her, did he? Where is he? I'll put him in his place."

"They are both in the parlour Sir. I only did as you requested."

"Not your fault if he turned out a scurvy knave. Bring a jug of ale. I want to speak to the girl."

There was another interruption. This time Louise was most surprised. Lady Belgower's voice sounded along the stone passage.

"George! What are you babbling about? Have you not yet seen the girl. Your friend Theobold says she is within." The harsh strident voice was impatient. "Take me to her."

"I prefer to see her alone first."

"Pshaw! You will only make a gudgeon of yourself! Leave it all to me. She will do as I say, or take the consequences!"

Louise shrank back in the inglenook. Even though she knew help was at hand she dreaded Lady Belgower's temper. The door opened and Lady Belgower stepped inside with George peering over her shoulder. She advanced into the room and paused to look down on Louise.

Louise did not need to act. She looked frightened. Lady Belgower smiled unpleasantly.

"So I have found you, my girl. Eloping with my nephew eh? Meaning to spend the night together, I warrant."

"You disgust me. You know that is not true!" Louise turned her head away to escape the baleful eyes.

"Look at me girl, when I am speaking to you. You will marry George or all London will know of this escapade, and you will be undone. Lord Falconer will not tolerate a besmirched bride."

"You expect me to marry George when I am already betrothed? You must be mad, Ma'am."

"You will be glad to, when society hears of this. Come, be a sensible girl and you can go to your bed and no harm done. Promise to break your betrothal to Lord Falconer, and marry George. Otherwise — " She stopped and smiled at George.

"Otherwise George will spend the night with you and we shall bring witnesses. There is young Mr Theobold. Fetch him in George. Let her see"

George reluctantly brought Mr Theobold in from the Tap-room. He gave Louise a grin.

"Hello Louise, are they giving you a bad time?"

"Oh Roland, she," pointing to Lady Belgower, "is trying to force an unwanted marriage onto me."

"I thought that was the game. Most uncivil of her. Do you want me to mill George down?" He put his arm about her. She had seen Lady Belgower's face change.

"What is the meaning of this? Do you know each other?"

"Of course. She is to be my sister-in-law. Did you not know?"

"But-but-George told me your name is Theobold."

Another voice broke in from the doorway.

"And it is indeed so Ma'am. Theobold is our family name." They all turned and Lord Falconer slowly came into the room and raised Louise's hand to his lips. "You are quite comfortable my dear?" She nodded wordlessly, too relieved to see him, but she managed a quivering smile.

Lady Belgower looked around at everybody there. And then she stamped her foot and screamed.

"You mutton-headed half-wit. Have

you ever done anything right?" Her hand came up and slapped George across the face. A red weal came up and he took a step back.

"Aunt, I did not know."

"Don't call me Aunt! Don't call me anything! Get out of my sight. And stay away from me. You! You!" She whirled on Louise. "And you, you sly bitch! You have been laughing at me. You must have known all the time. I could strangle you!"

She rushed over to Louise, hands outstretched like claws. Lord Falconer caught her by the shoulder and she swung round, raking the side of his face. Blood gushed from the deep scratches and Louise cried out in alarm.

"A mere nothing," murmured Lord Falconer. "Do not distress yourself." And then he addressed himself to Lady Belgower. "Have you quite finished?" They stared at each other, and Lady Belgower's eyes fell. "Then hear me out. One word of this repeated anywhere, and I mean anywhere and I shall see to it that everything about you is made public. Your part in this affair will debar you from society for life. Do you understand?" She did not answer.

Roland helped Louise out of the inglenook and picked up her belongings. "Ready?" he smiled. "Then let us go."

"I will take her, Roland," said his Lordship. "You stay to pay the reckoning," and led the way outside to the waiting coach. As they walked over the cobbles they could hear sounds of hysteria within. They paused before climbing into the coach and Louise turned to face him.

"So it's all over, thanks to you Marcus. I was so very frightened. Oh Marcus, if I had married that horrible man." She buried her head into his chest. He kissed her gently.

"It is over. Forget it. We have more important things to think about. Our marriage for instance."

"Oh Marcus, then you do not really think I was a straw damsel? You were so angry."

"Hush, my precious. I never really did

think so. At least after I got over my temper and knew you better. But you were a little minx."

"Just because you hurt my pride."

Roland came out of the inn, laughing. "What! Standing freezing outside the coach! You should have been aboard by now. A man in love has more hair than wit! Get her inside man, and then you can kiss her to your heart's content!"

He mounted the box and took the reins, and the ostler was ready to jump back on the first bound, when the innkeeper ran out of the inn, waving his arms.

"Wait wait. Who pays the reckoning?"

"The gentleman inside. He will pay your shot. It is his day of reckoning!" He laughed again at the look of bewilderment on the part of the innkeeper, and then jerked his reins and the ostler sprang away just in time. The horses started at a gallop and they turned out of the cobbled yard, nearly taking the gatepost with them.

The horses straightened out and went

at a headlong gallop and Roland let out a hunting yell.

"Yoicks and tallyho!" Then he rapped on the trapdoor of the coach. Marcus opened it and Roland looked down, "All's well inside? Then take a good hold of her, we're bound for London Town and we are going to break records!"

"No need for that dear boy. We have all night to get home. Take the long way round Roland. I may do you a favour someday!"

TIME FOR LOVING
Kathleen Treves

When two young men are saved from their capsized boat and brought to Honeybank Farm House to recover, their arrival causes upheavals in the family, and Deborah has to cope with many problems until she finds time for loving!

THE SPOTTED PLUME
Yvonne Whittal

"I can only stand females in small doses," the arrogant Hunter Maynard told Jennifer. That was alright by Jennifer, her career as a nurse would come first in her life. Or would it?

SURGEON'S SECOND WIFE
Kay Winchester

A widower for some years, Senior Surgeon Nicholas Kent's life changes when he literally bumps into eighteen year old Venny.

Ca
ar
lo
h
tl

T
s
r
w
h
v

M
p
u
s
s

h
't
ve
et

it
ot
le
ds
ow
y.

a
ut
lle
tic

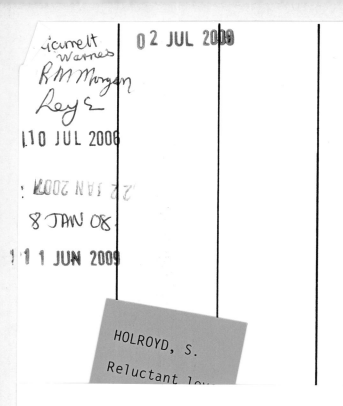